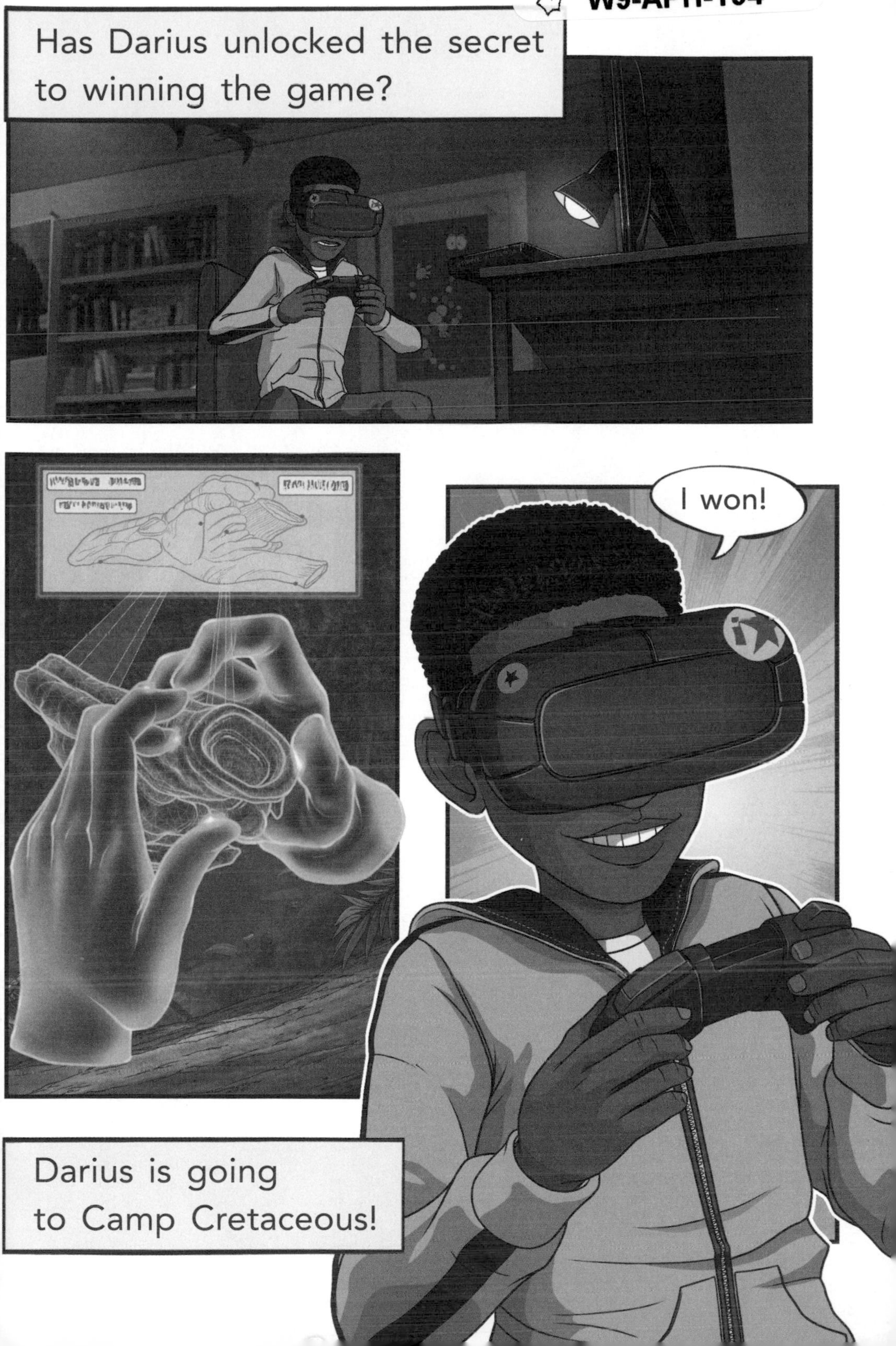
Has Darius unlocked the secret to winning the game?
I won!
Darius is going to Camp Cretaceous!

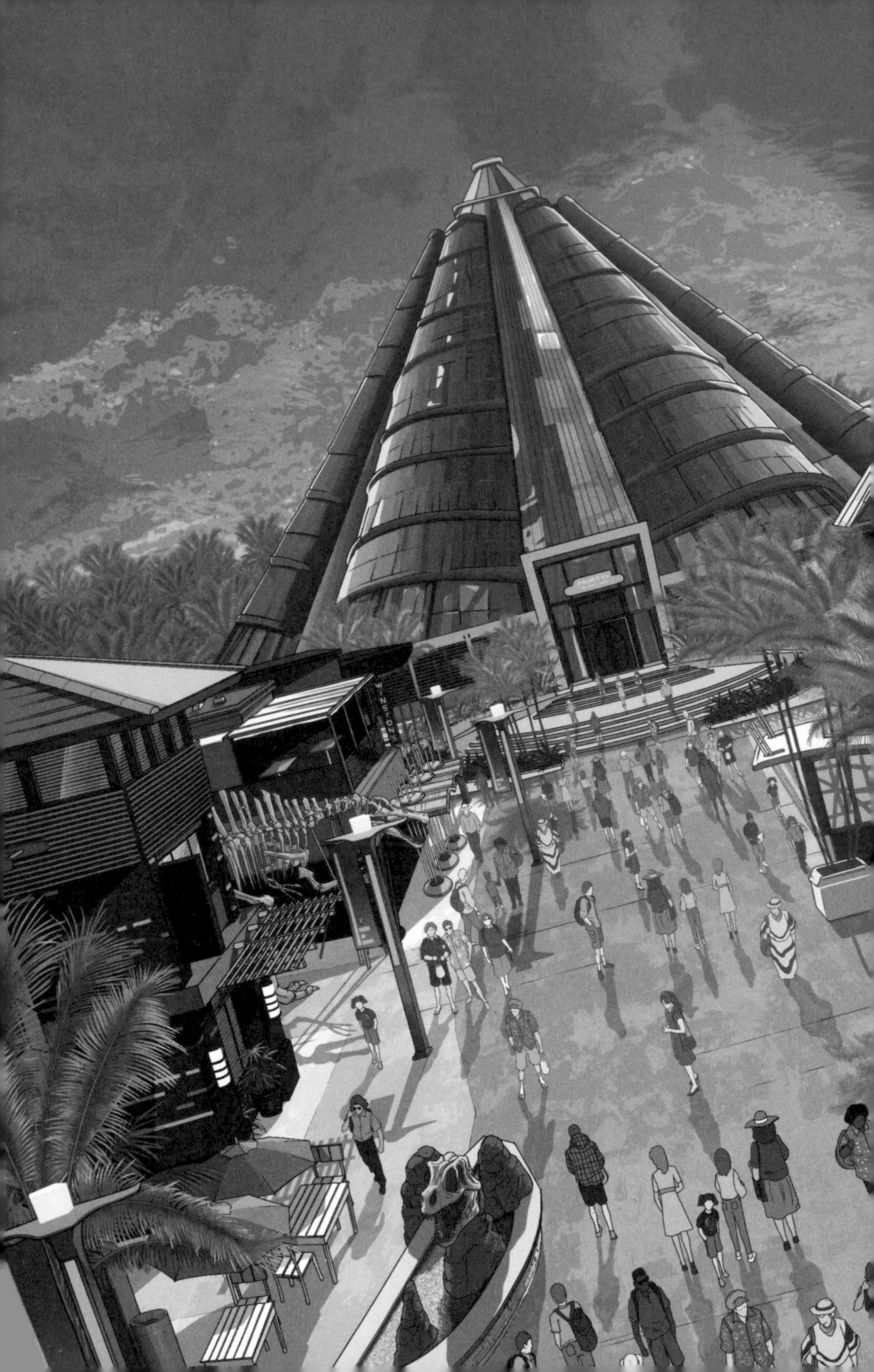
WINSTONS

Dear Parent:

Psst . . . you're looking at the Super Secret Weapon of Reading. It's called comics.

STEP INTO READING® COMIC READERS are a perfect step in learning to read. They provide visual cues to the meaning of words and helpfully break out short pieces of dialogue into speech balloons.

Here are some terms commonly associated with comics:

PANEL: A section of a comic with a box drawn around it.
CAPTION: Narration that helps set the scene.
SPEECH BALLOON: A bubble containing dialogue.
GUTTER: The space between panels.

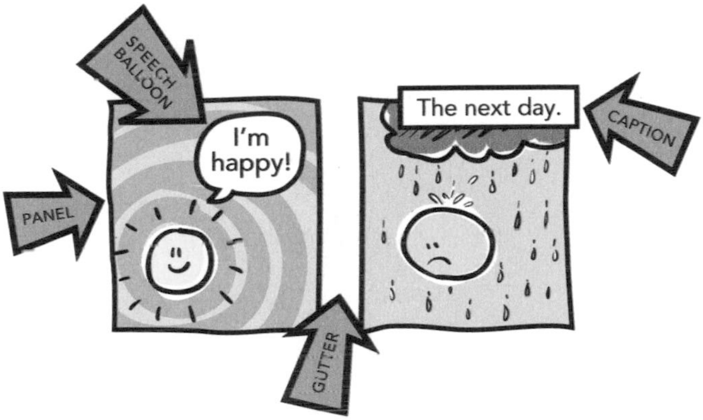

SPEECH BALLOON
I'm happy!
PANEL
The next day.
CAPTION
GUTTER

Tips for reading comics with your child:

- **Have your child read the speech balloons while you read the captions.**
- **Ask your child: What is a character feeling? How can you tell?**
- **Have your child draw a comic showing what happens after the book is finished.**

STEP INTO READING® COMIC READERS are designed to engage and to provide an empowering reading experience. They are also fun. The best-kept secret of comics is that they create lifelong readers. **And that will make you the real hero of the story!**

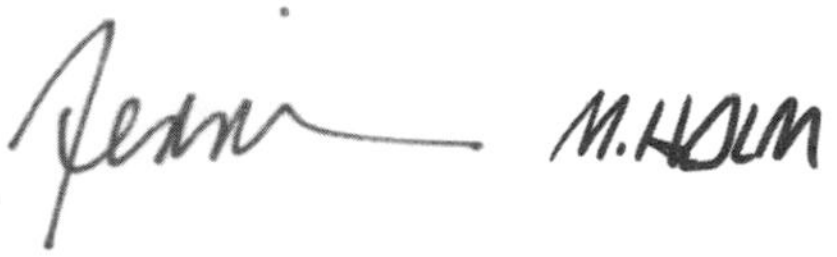

Jennifer L. Holm and Matthew Holm
Co-creators of the Babymouse and Squish series

All Rights Reserved. Published in the United States by Random House Children's Books, a division of Penguin Random House LLC, 1745 Broadway, New York, NY 10019, and in Canada by Penguin Random House Canada Limited, Toronto. Step into Reading, Random House, and the Random House colophon are registered trademarks of Penguin Random House LLC.

Visit us on the Web!
StepIntoReading.com
rhcbooks.com

Educators and librarians, for a variety of teaching tools, visit us at RHTeachersLibrarians.com

ISBN 978-0-593-30335-1 (trade)—ISBN 978-0-593-30336-8 (lib. bdg.)—
ISBN 978-0-593-30337-5 (ebook)

Printed in the United States of America 10 9 8 7 6 5 4 3 2 1

Random House Children's Books supports the First Amendment and celebrates the right to read.

STEP INTO READING®

STEP 3

READING ON YOUR OWN

A COMIC READER

JURASSIC WORLD

CAMP CRETACEOUS

WELCOME TO CAMP!

adapted by Steve Behling

illustrated by Patrick Spaziante

Random House 🏠 New York

The Jurassic World video game
is full of dinosaurs!
The first player to beat the game
wins a very special prize.

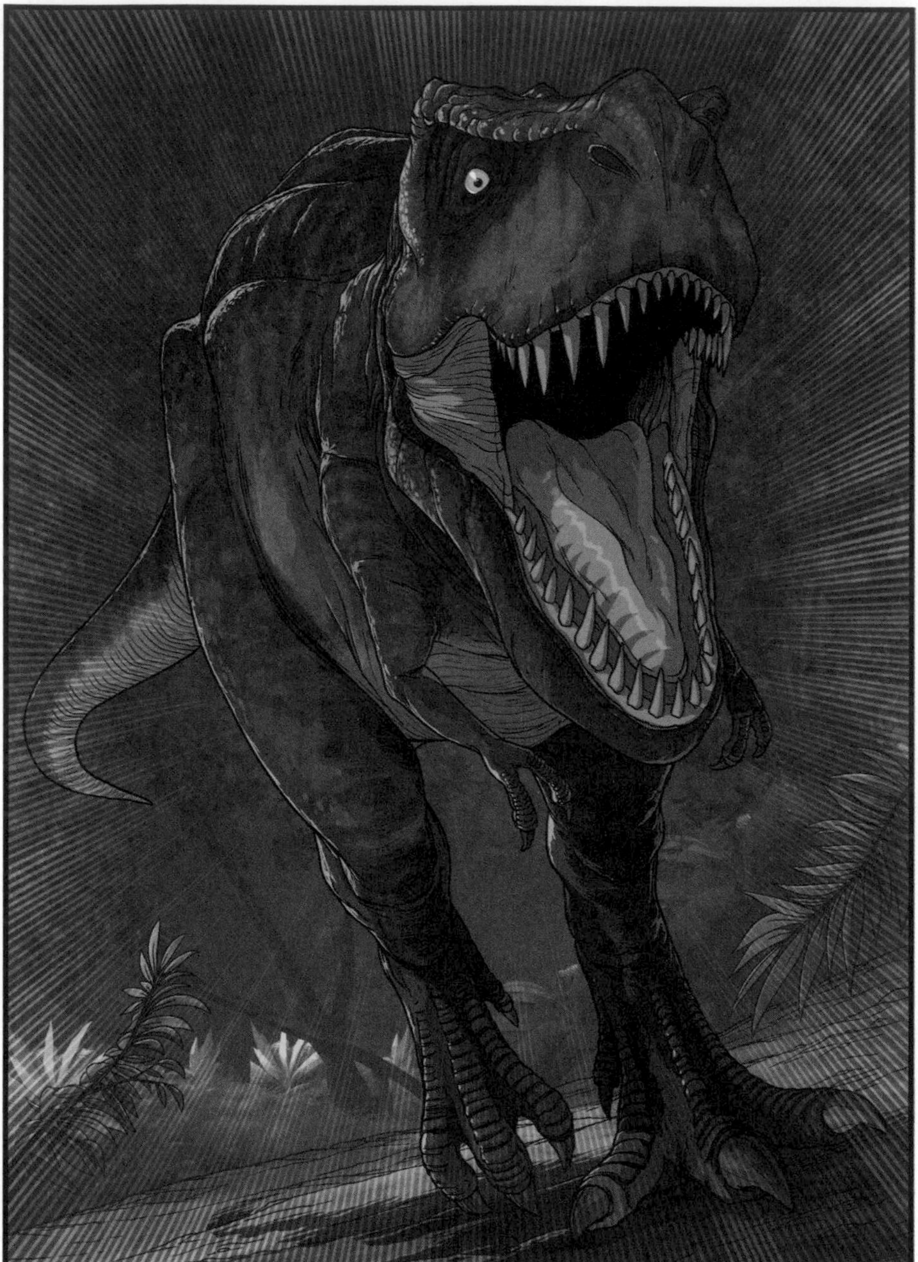

Camp Cretaceous is a camp
for kids at Jurassic World.
Darius can't believe it.
He's going to an island
with real live dinosaurs!

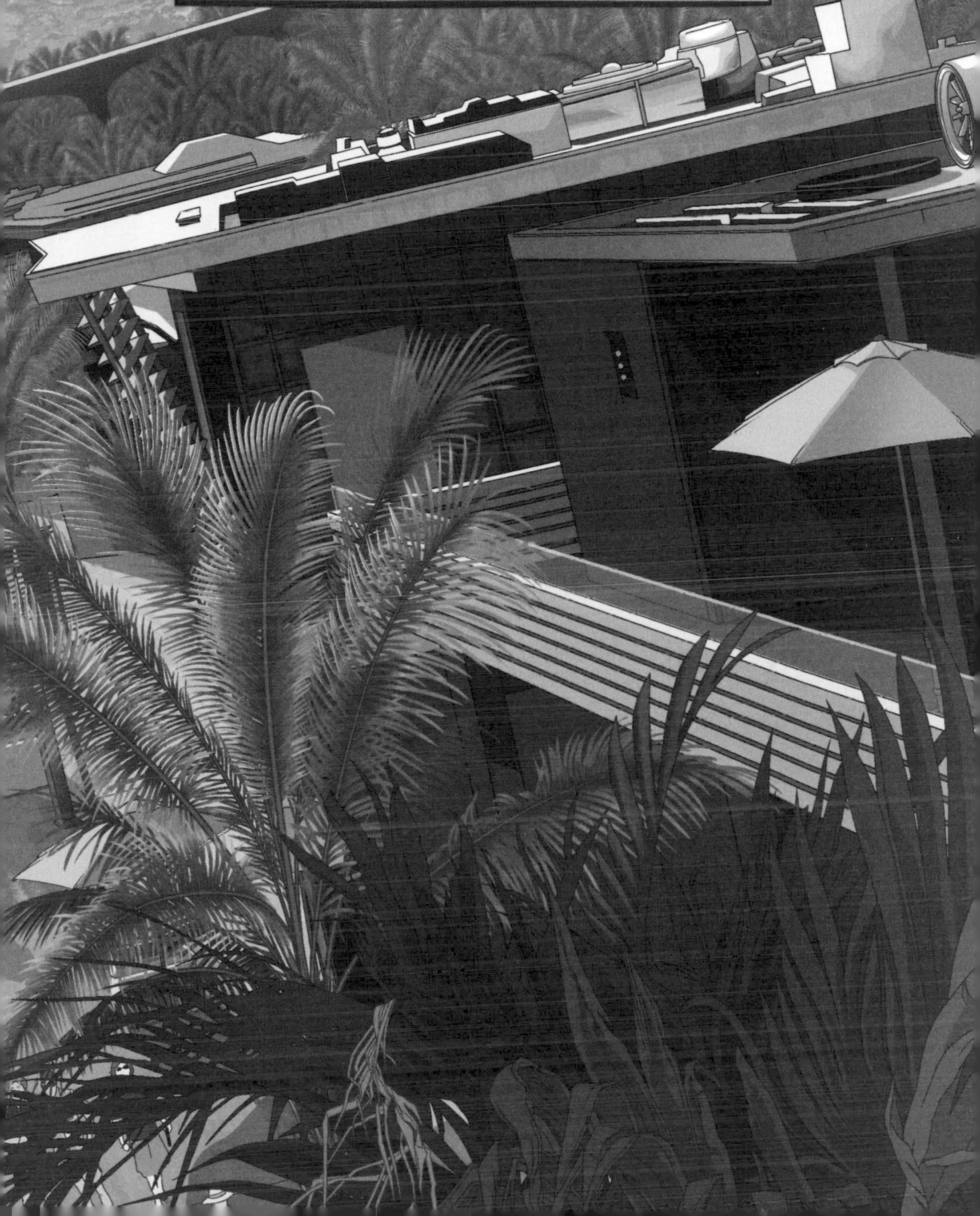

Darius is super excited!
First, he meets his camp counselors,
Roxie and Dave.
Then he meets his fellow campers.

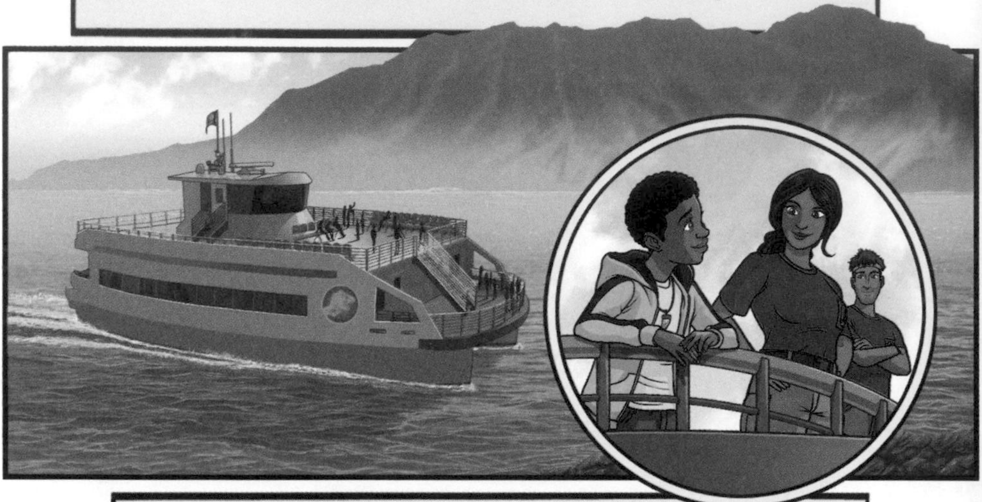

There's Brooklynn, Sammy,
Yasmina, and Ben.
Kenji arrives by helicopter.
He acts like he owns the place.

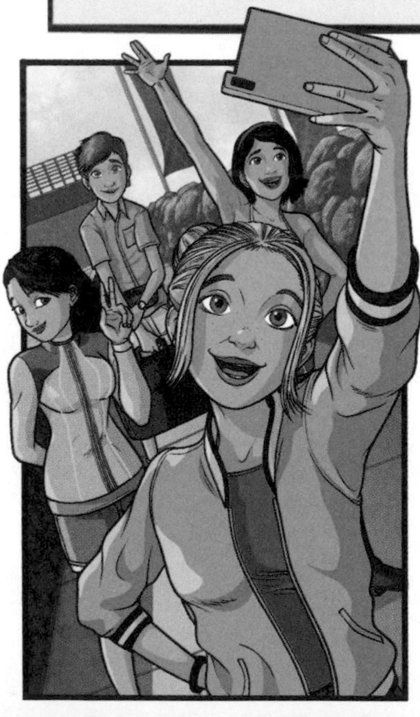

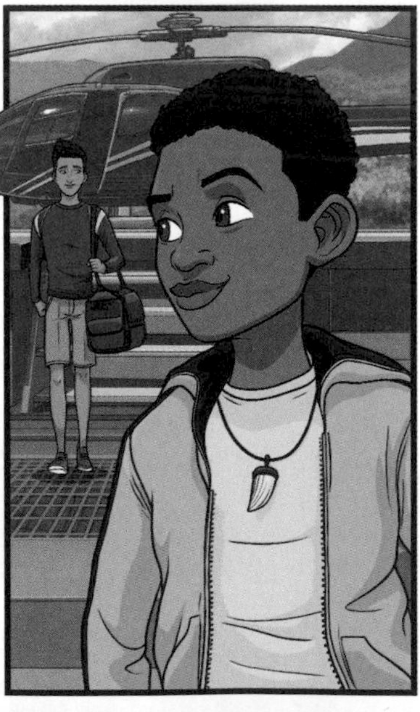

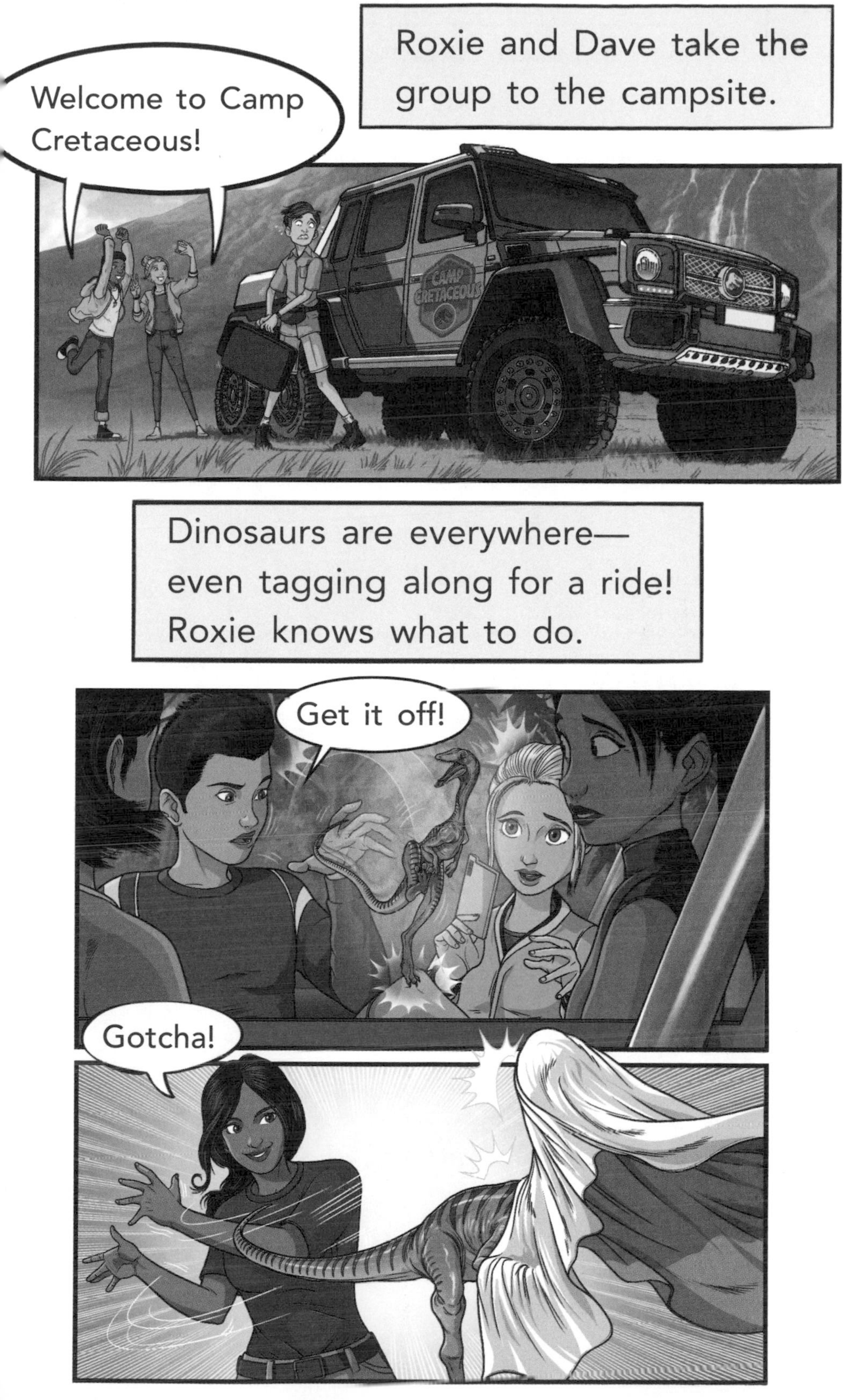
Roxie and Dave take the group to the campsite.
Welcome to Camp Cretaceous!
Camp Cretaceous
Dinosaurs are everywhere—even tagging along for a ride! Roxie knows what to do.
Get it off!
Gotcha!

At last, the kids arrive at Camp Cretaceous! Darius can't wait to explore.

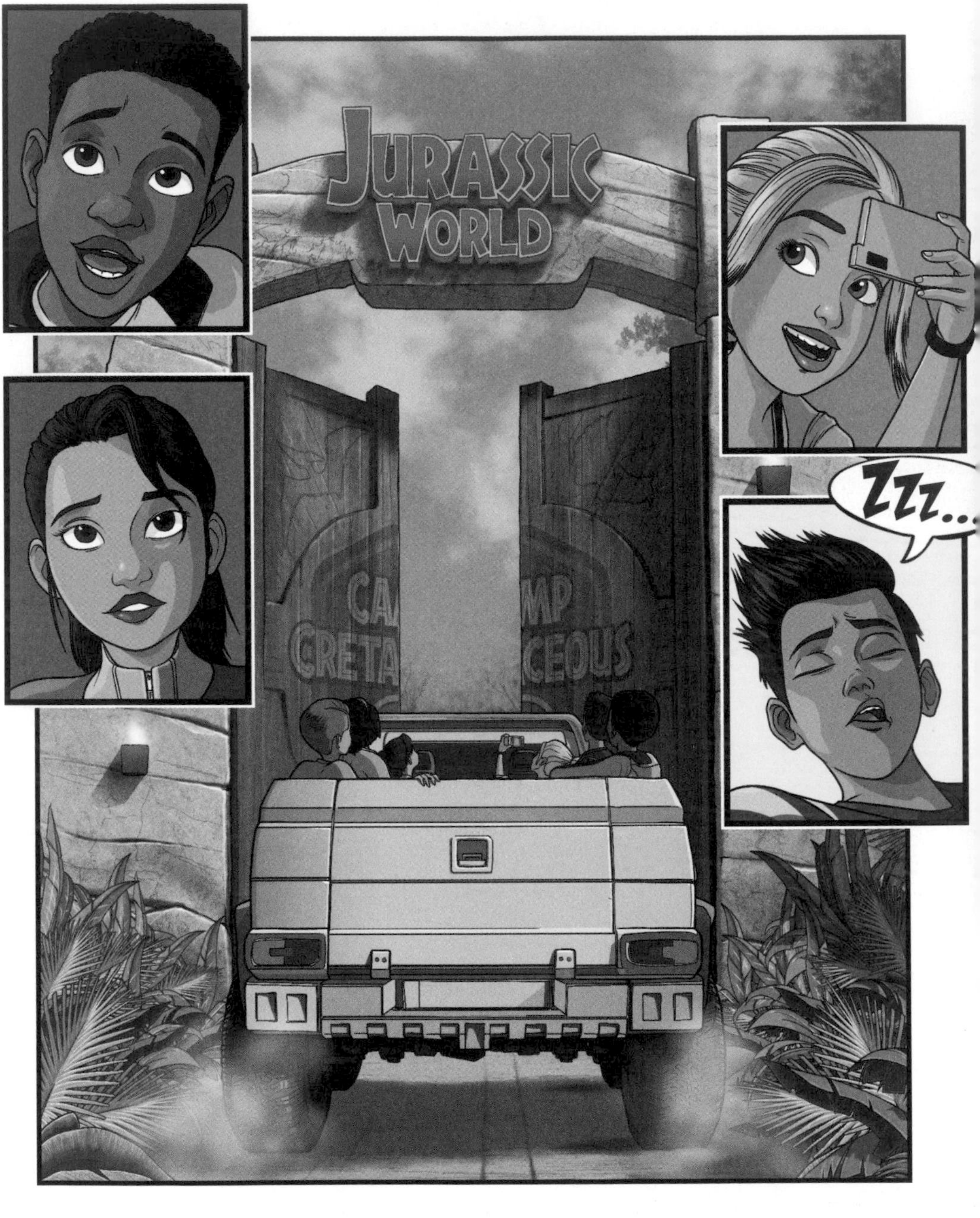
JURASSIC WORLD
CA MP
CRETA CEOUS
ZZZ...

The kids stay in a really nice tree house.
Darius thinks it's cool!
Kenji doesn't.

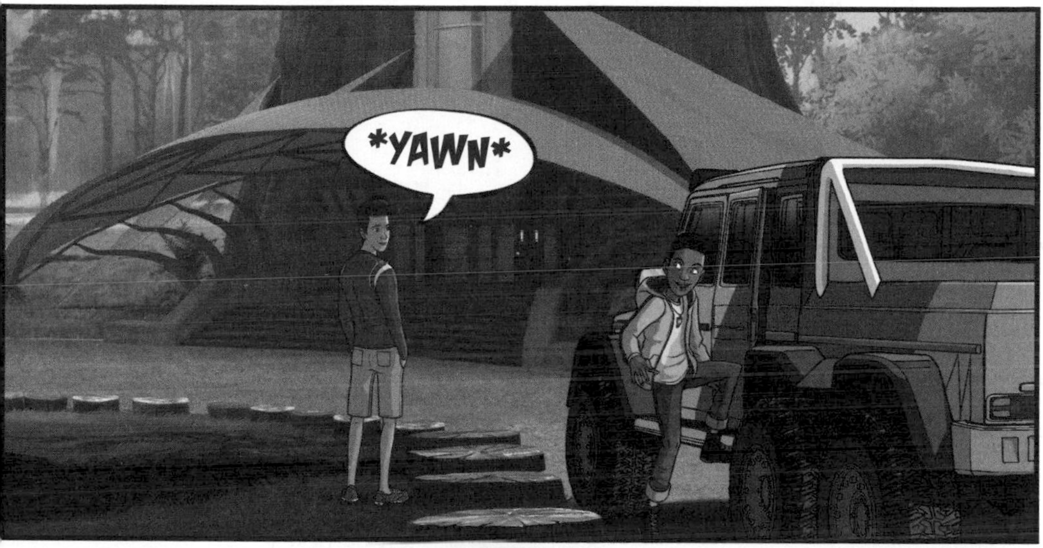
YAWN

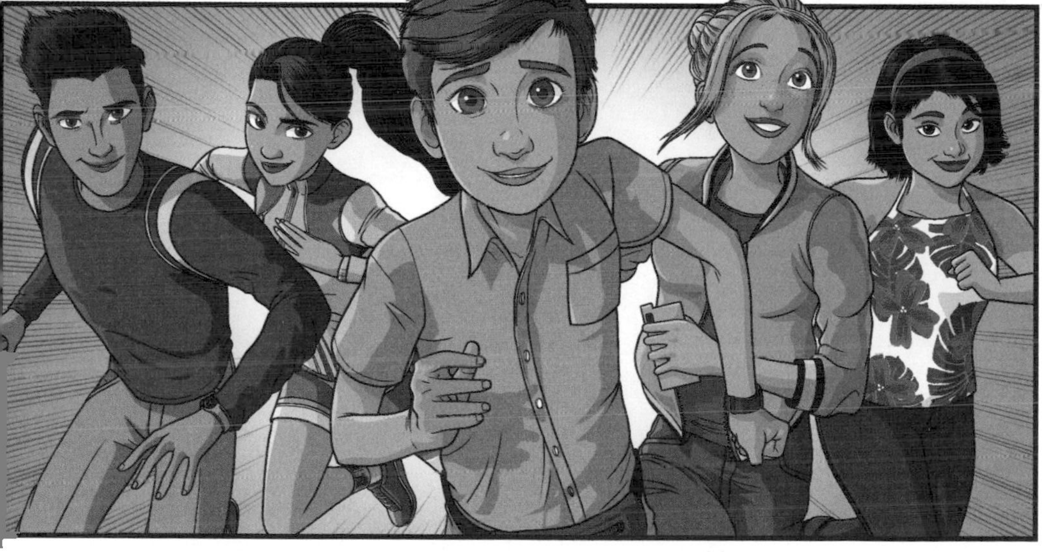

The kids race for the elevator.
They each want to get the best room . . .

. . . and the top bunk!
Everyone's there except Darius.

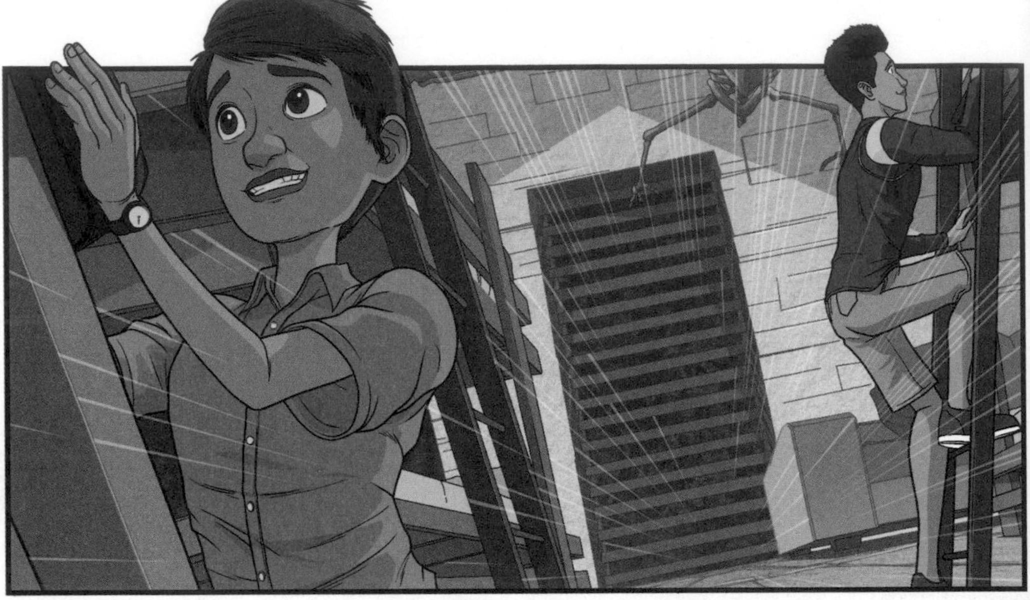

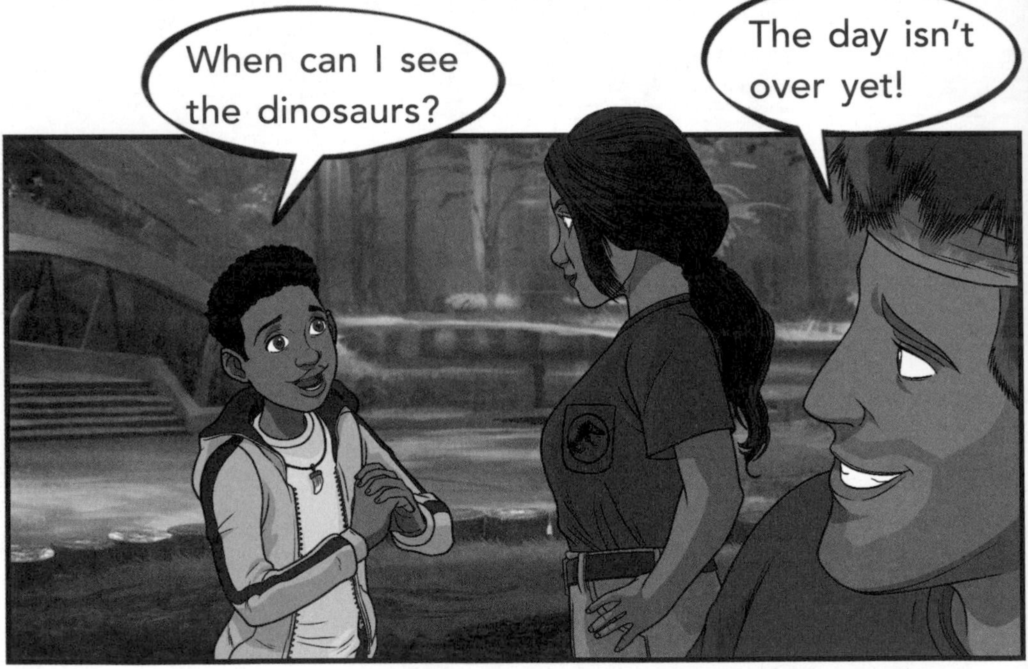
When can I see the dinosaurs?
The day isn't over yet!

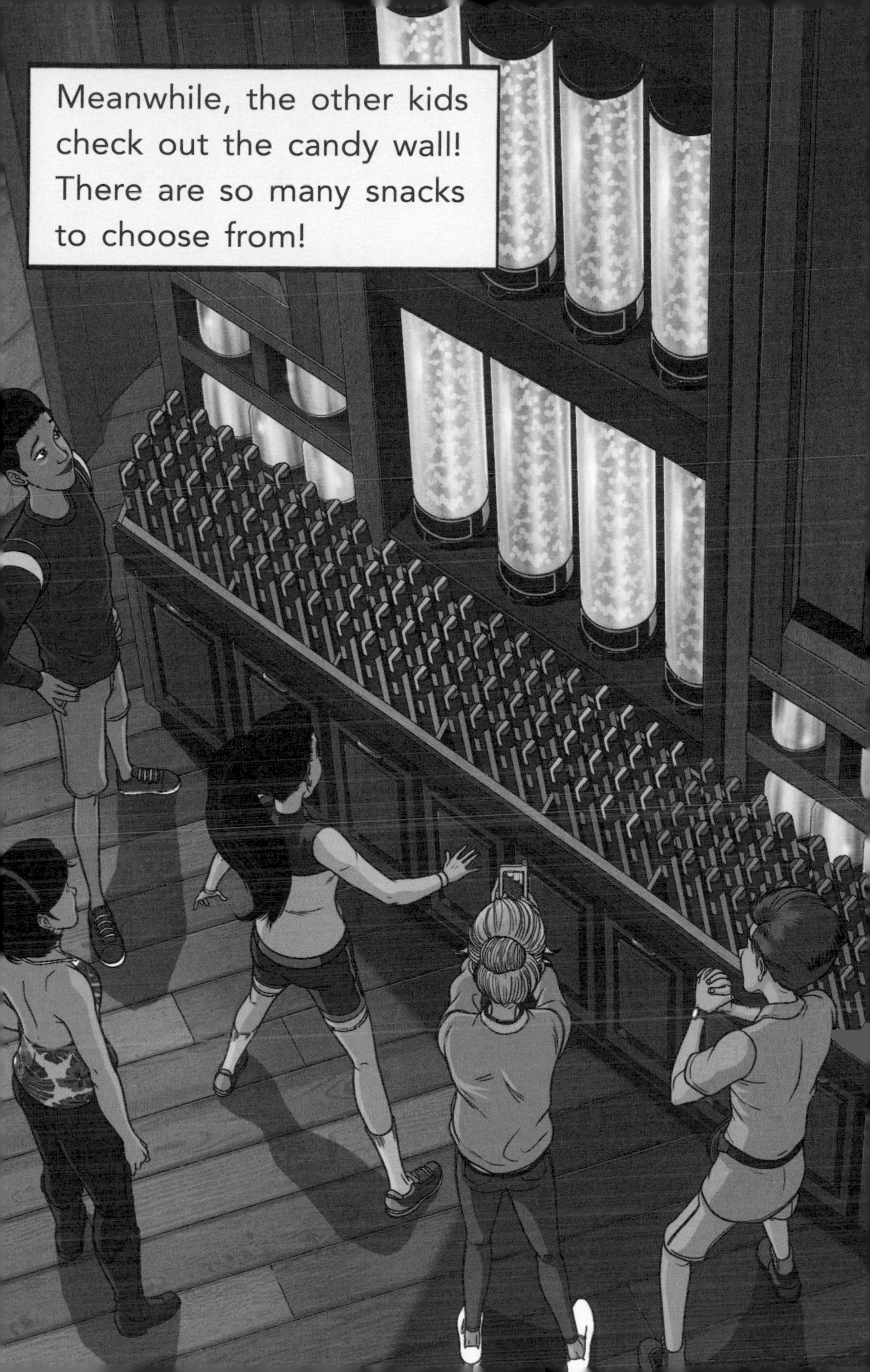
Meanwhile, the other kids check out the candy wall! There are so many snacks to choose from!

There are three rules to follow at Camp Cretaceous.

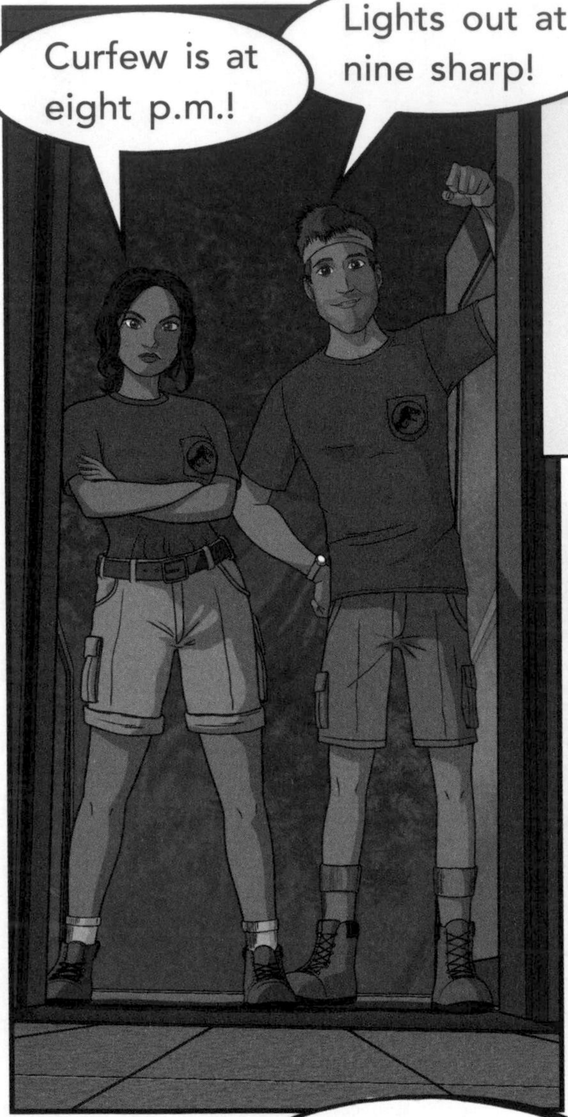
Curfew is at eight p.m.!
Lights out at nine sharp!

The third and most important rule is that you must always keep your distance from the dinosaurs.

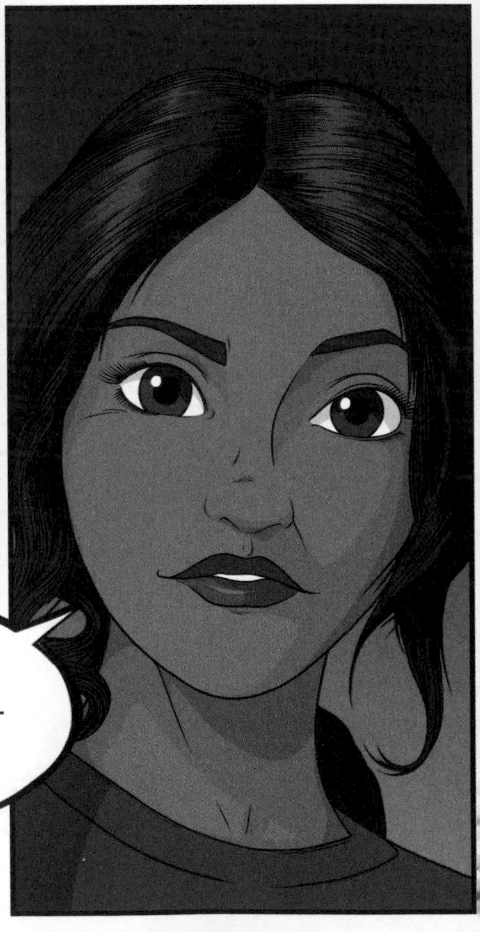
You could be seriously hurt—if not worse.

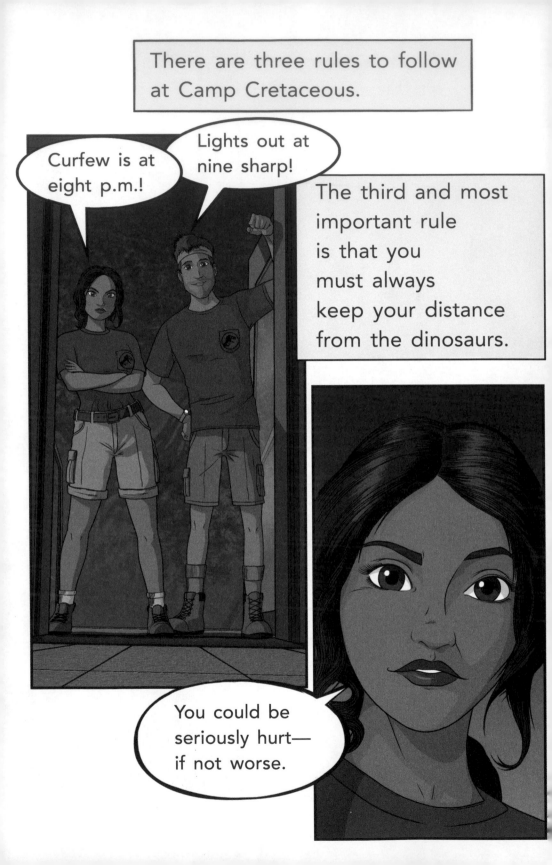

Now that they know the rules, the kids go for a ride.

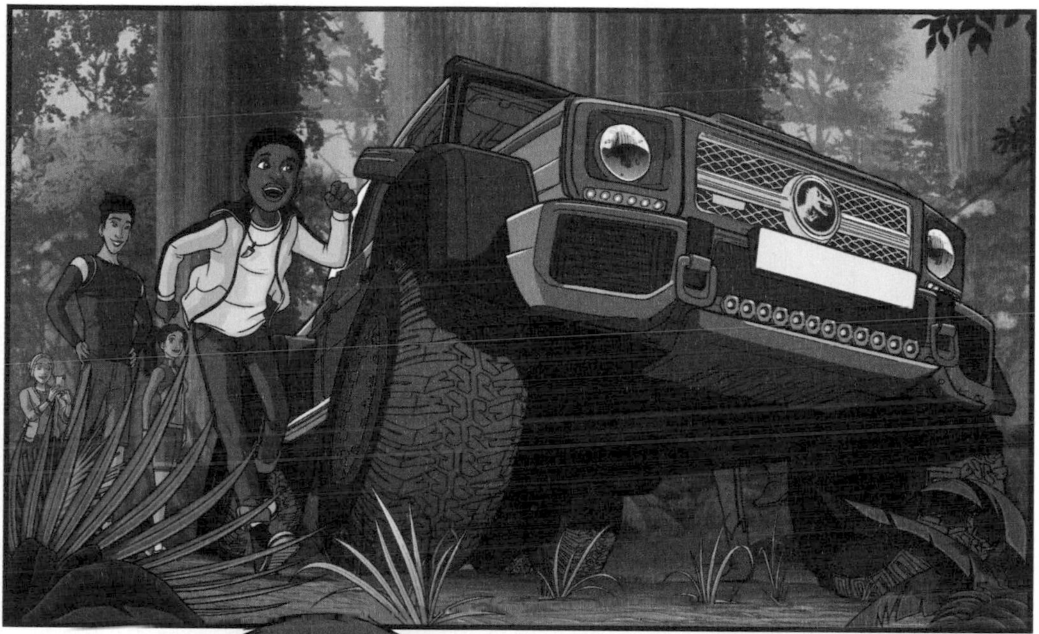

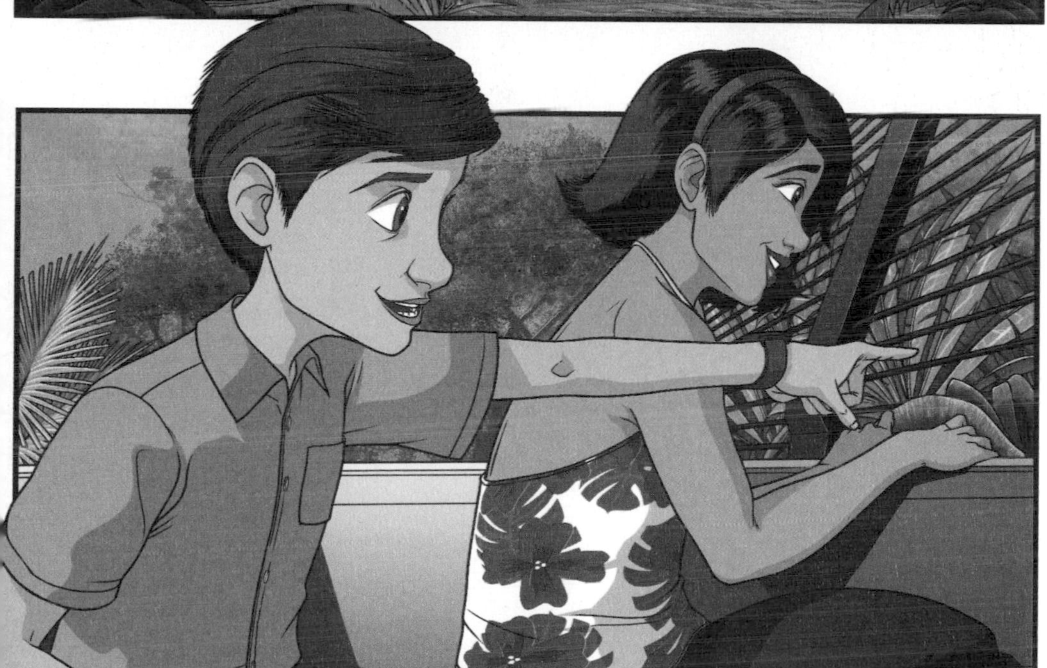

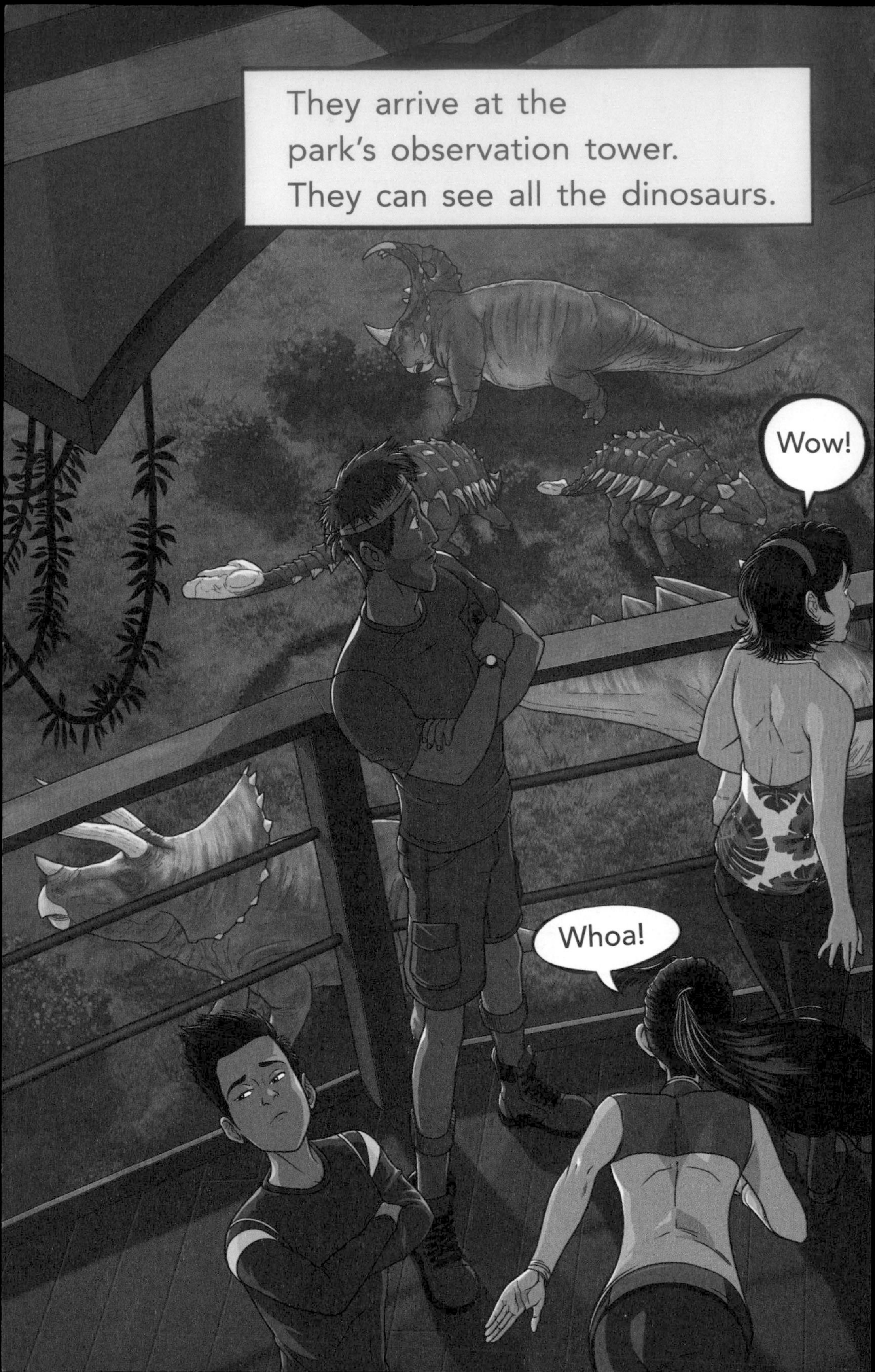
They arrive at the park's observation tower. They can see all the dinosaurs.
Wow!
Whoa!

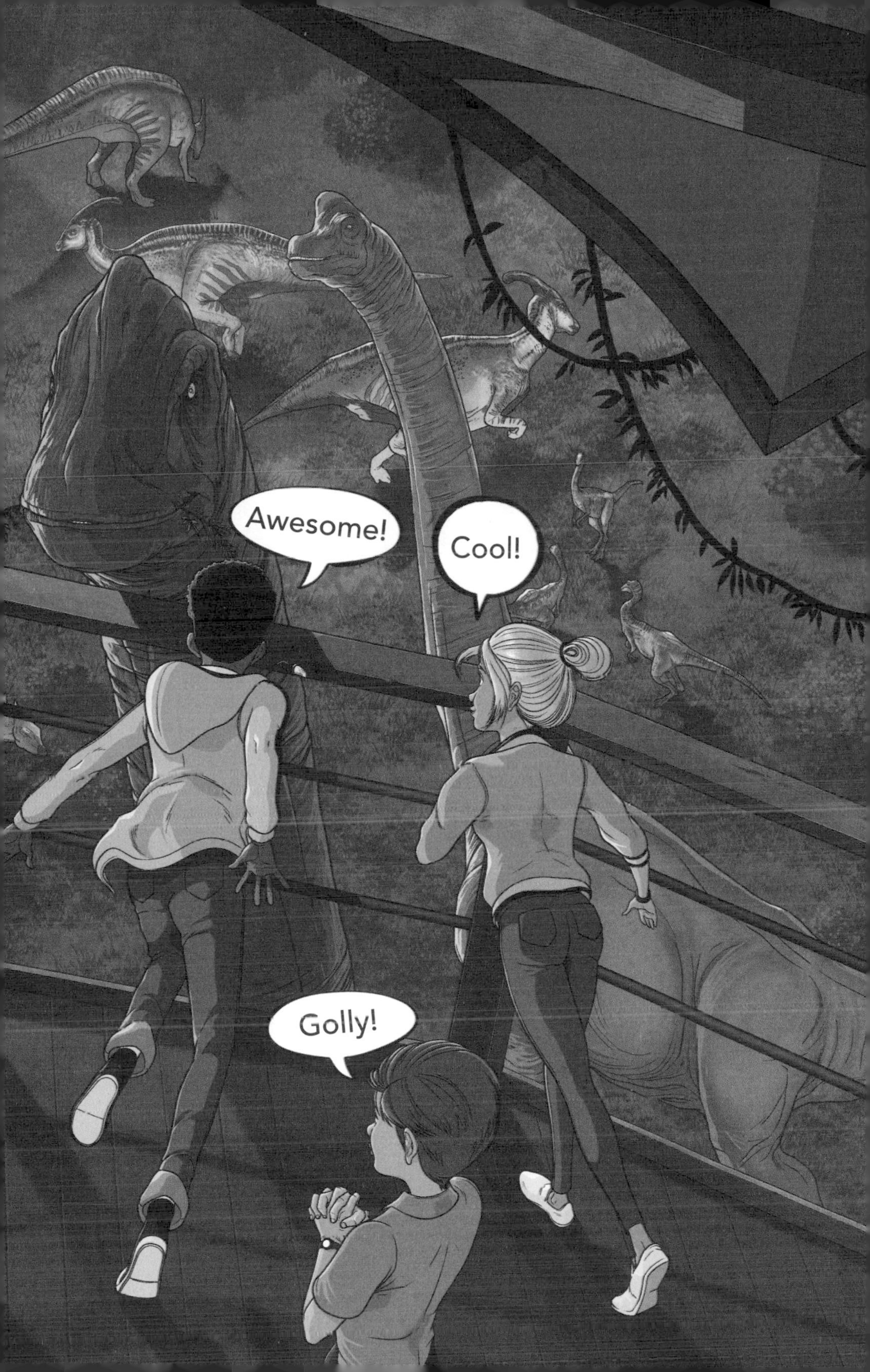
Awesome!
Cool!
Golly!

Darius sees a Parasaurolophus and a Brachiosaurus.

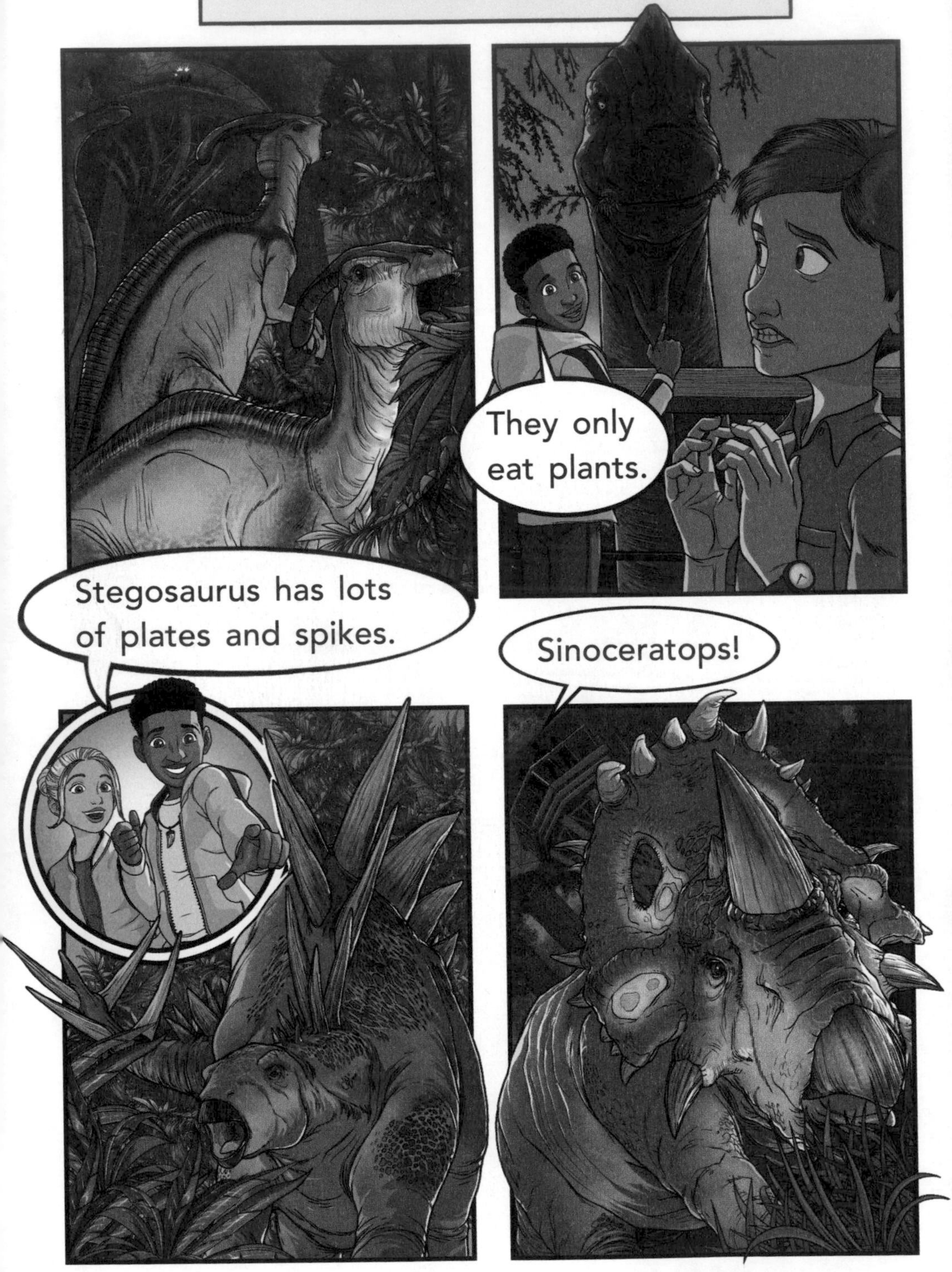
They only eat plants.
Stegosaurus has lots of plates and spikes.
Sinoceratops!

The kids take the zipline
down to the jungle.
It's super fast—and super fun!

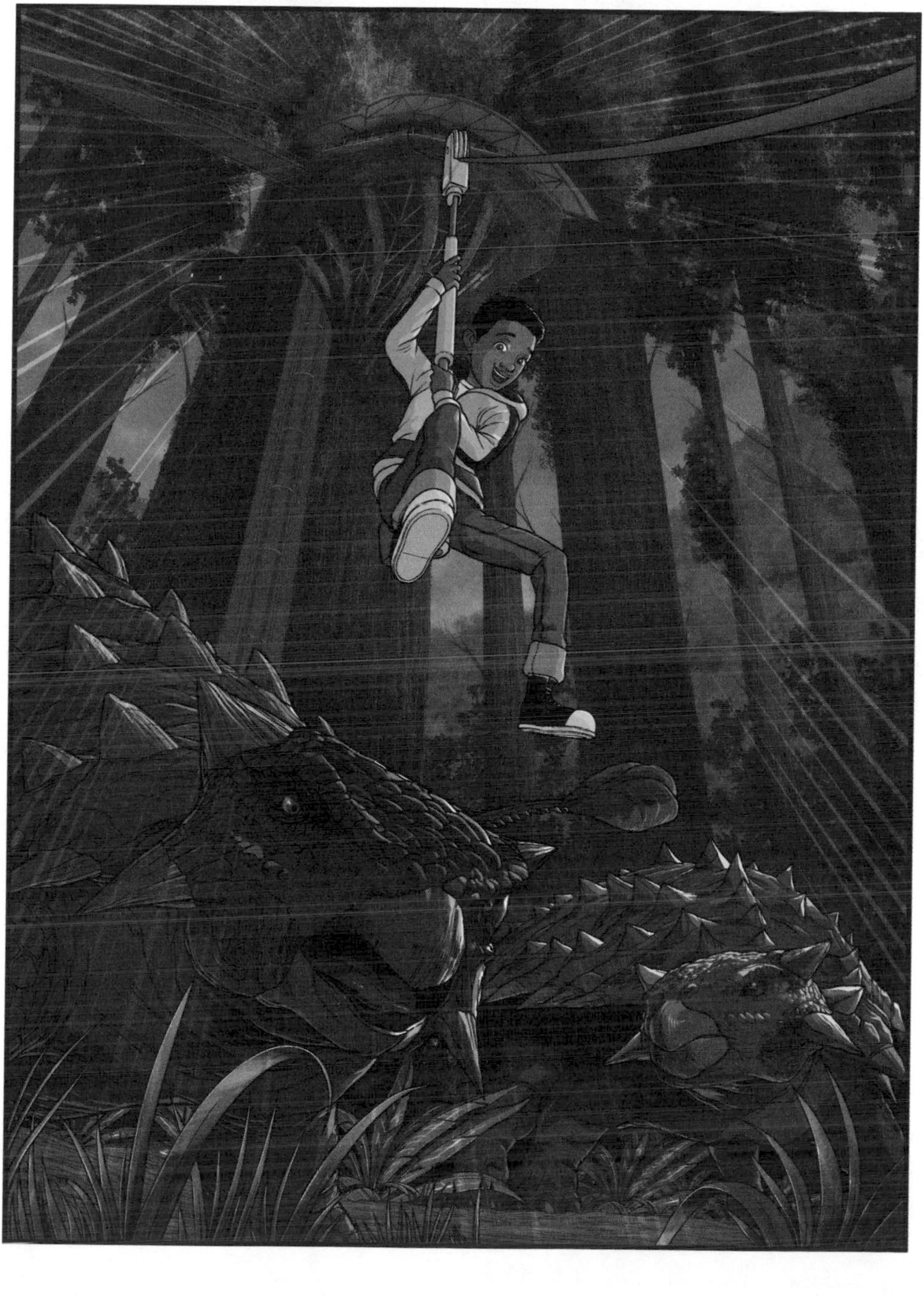

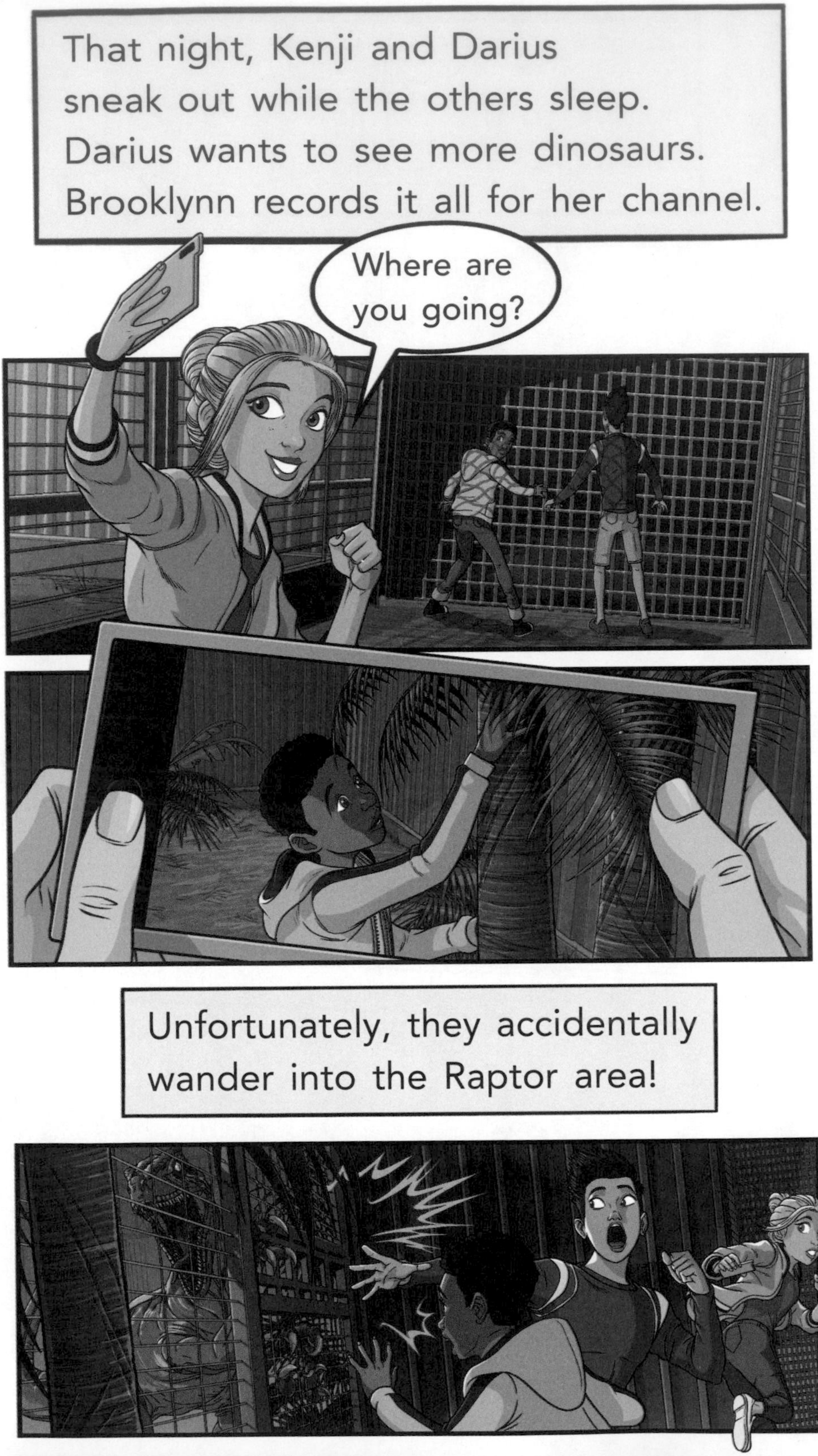
That night, Kenji and Darius sneak out while the others sleep. Darius wants to see more dinosaurs. Brooklynn records it all for her channel.
Where are you going?
Unfortunately, they accidentally wander into the Raptor area!

Brooklynn presses a button
to help them escape.
There's just one problem—

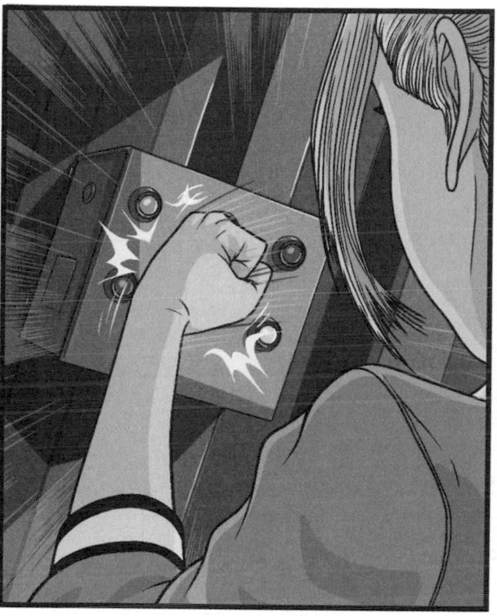

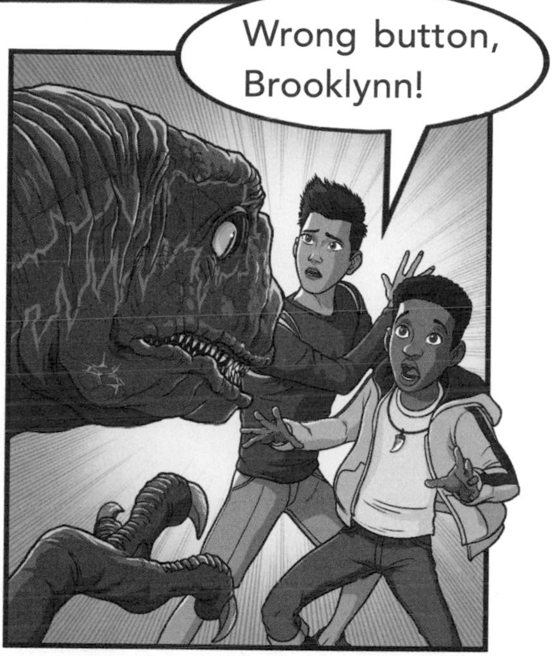
Wrong button, Brooklynn!

Darius looks around
for something
to help them get out.
Roxie and Dave arrive
to help!
They throw meat
into the Raptors' pen.

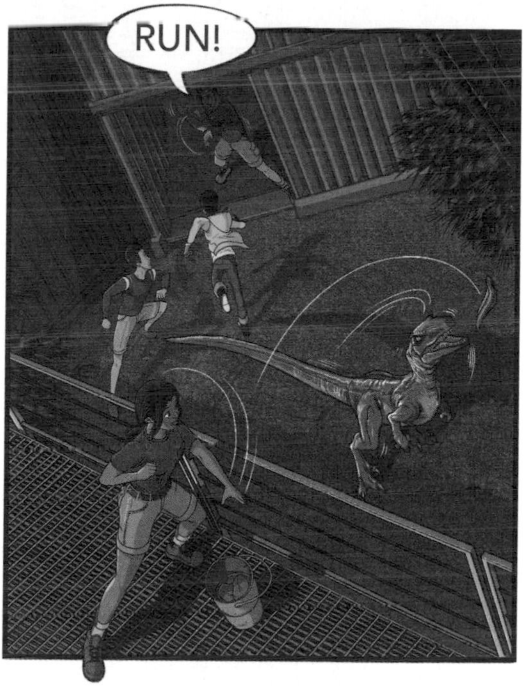
RUN!

The counselors are glad the kids are safe.
But they're also mad!
They caught the boys breaking the rules.

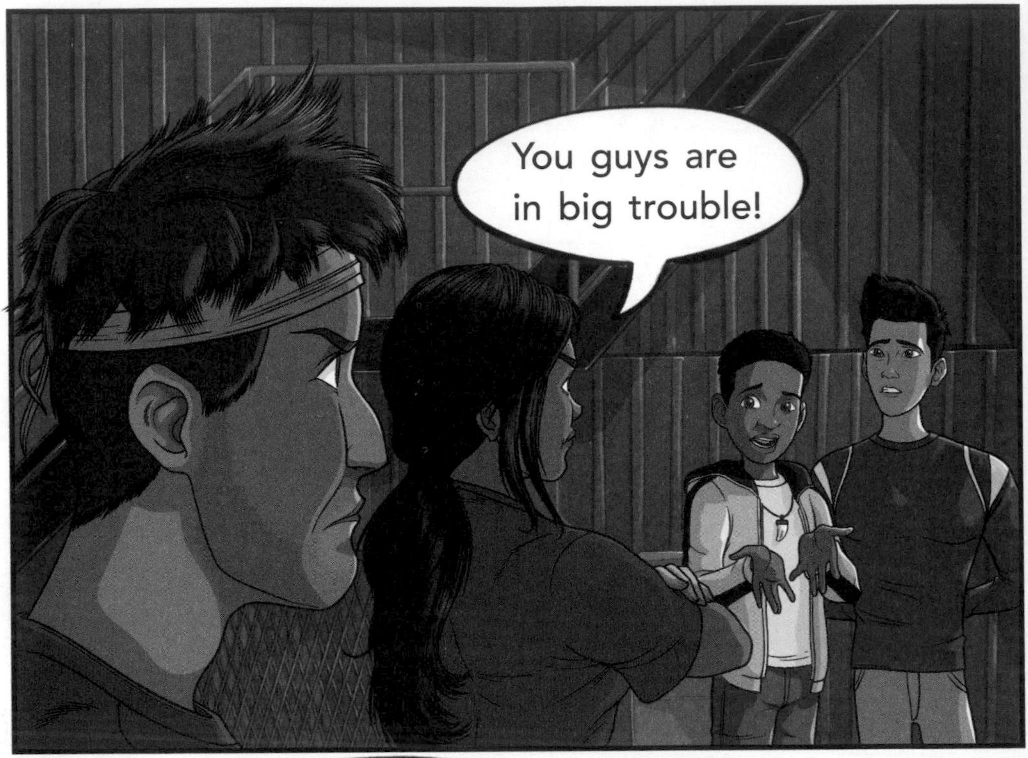
You guys are in big trouble!

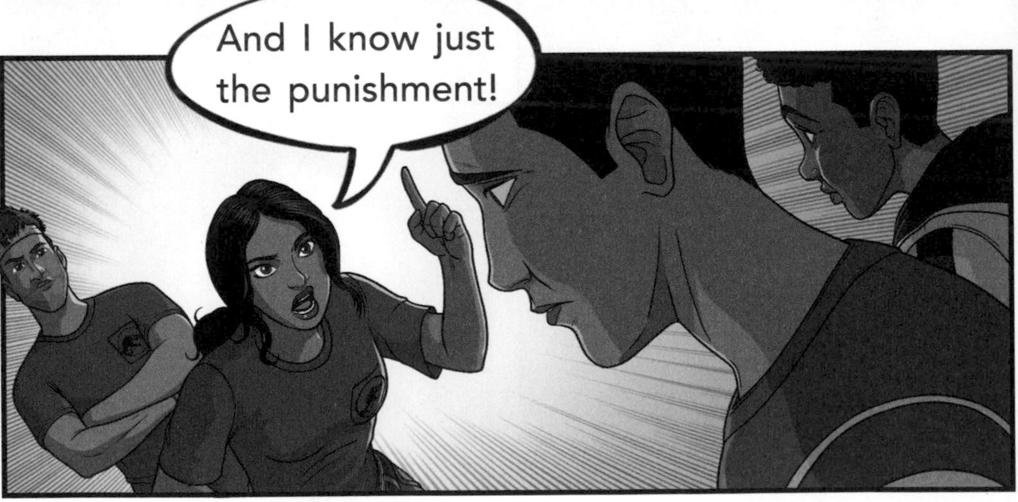
And I know just the punishment!

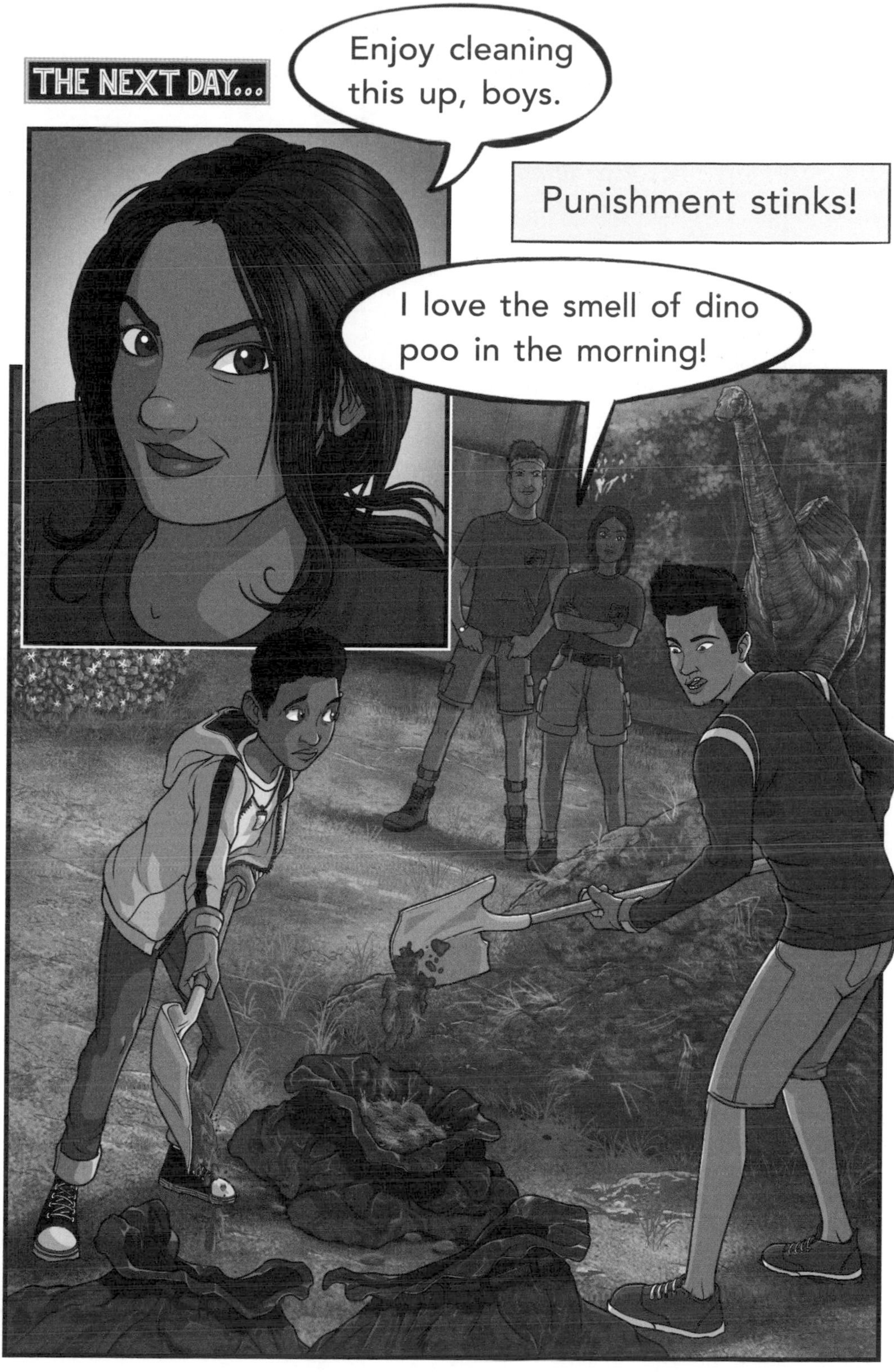
THE NEXT DAY...
Enjoy cleaning this up, boys.
Punishment stinks!
I love the smell of dino poo in the morning!

Darius and Kenji will miss
the trip to the genetics lab.
That's where dinosaurs are made!
The other kids go inside.

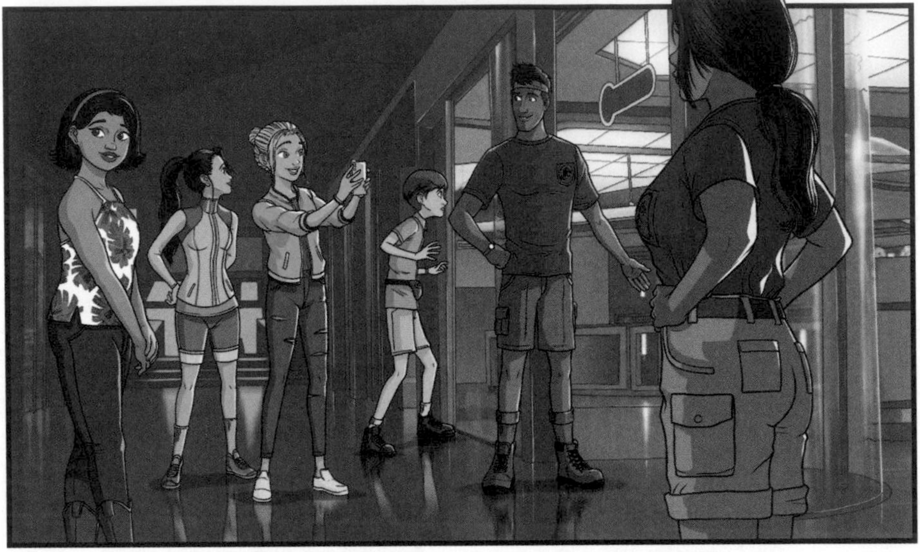

The scientists are very busy.
Making dinosaurs isn't easy!

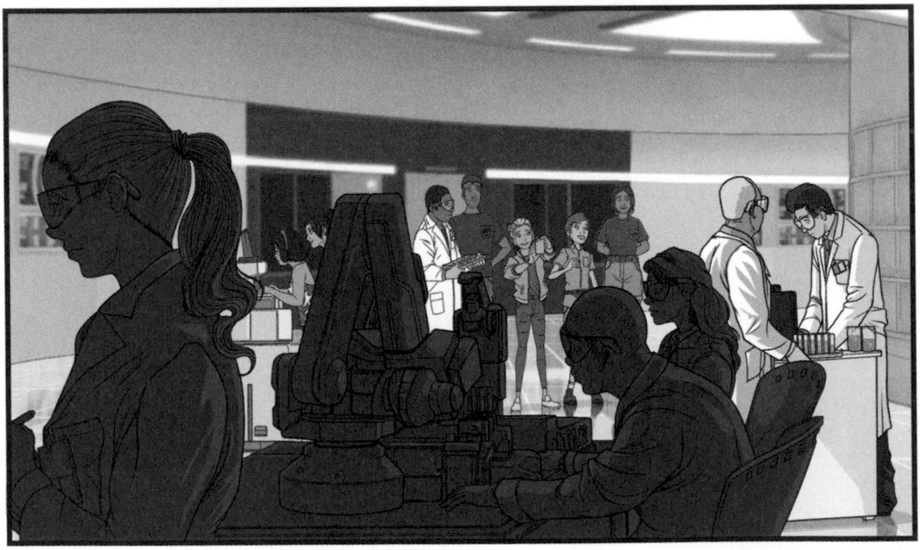

The kids meet Dr. Wu.
He's in charge of the lab.
He doesn't have time for campers.
Brooklynn has a way with people, though.

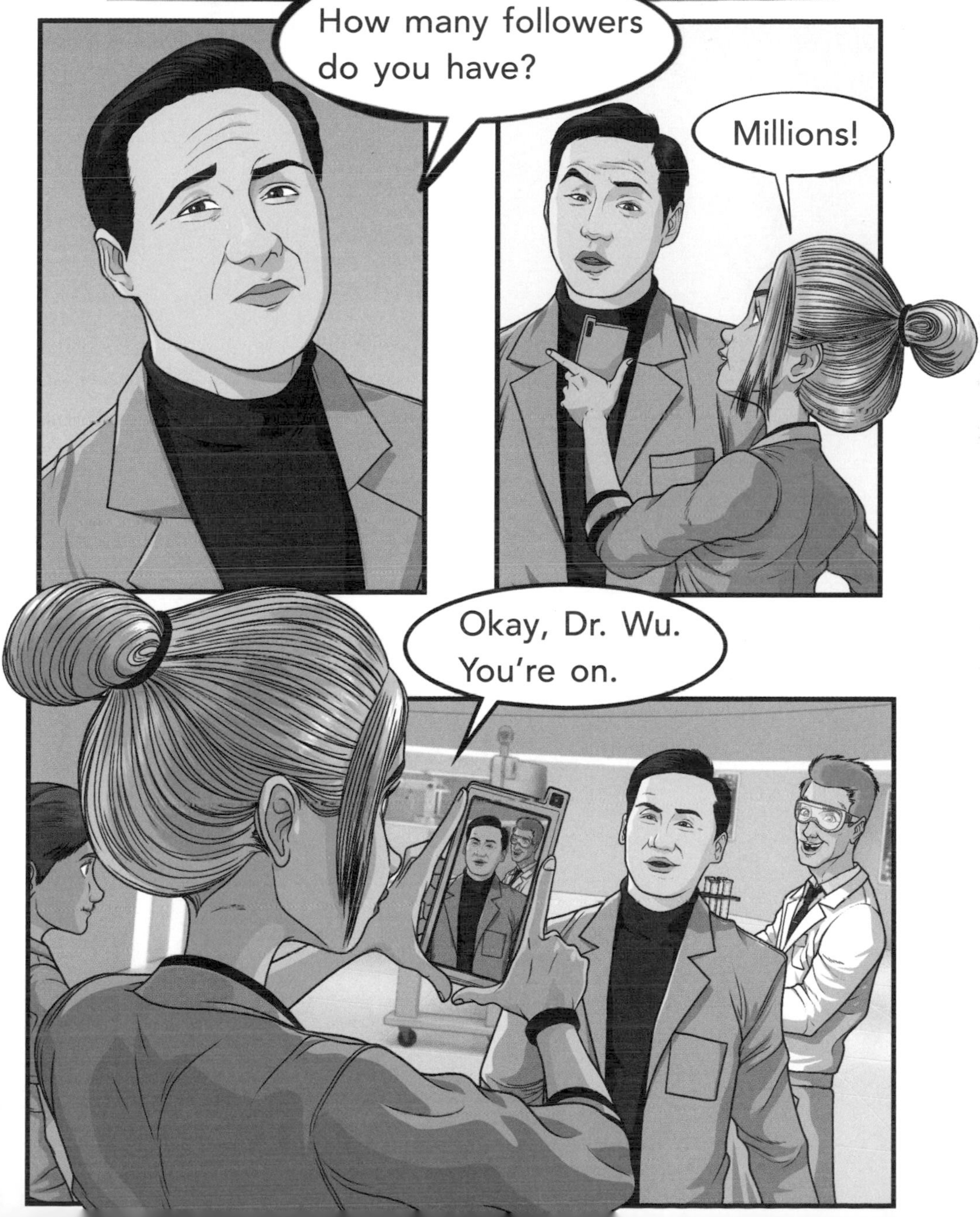
How many followers do you have?
Millions!
Okay, Dr. Wu. You're on.

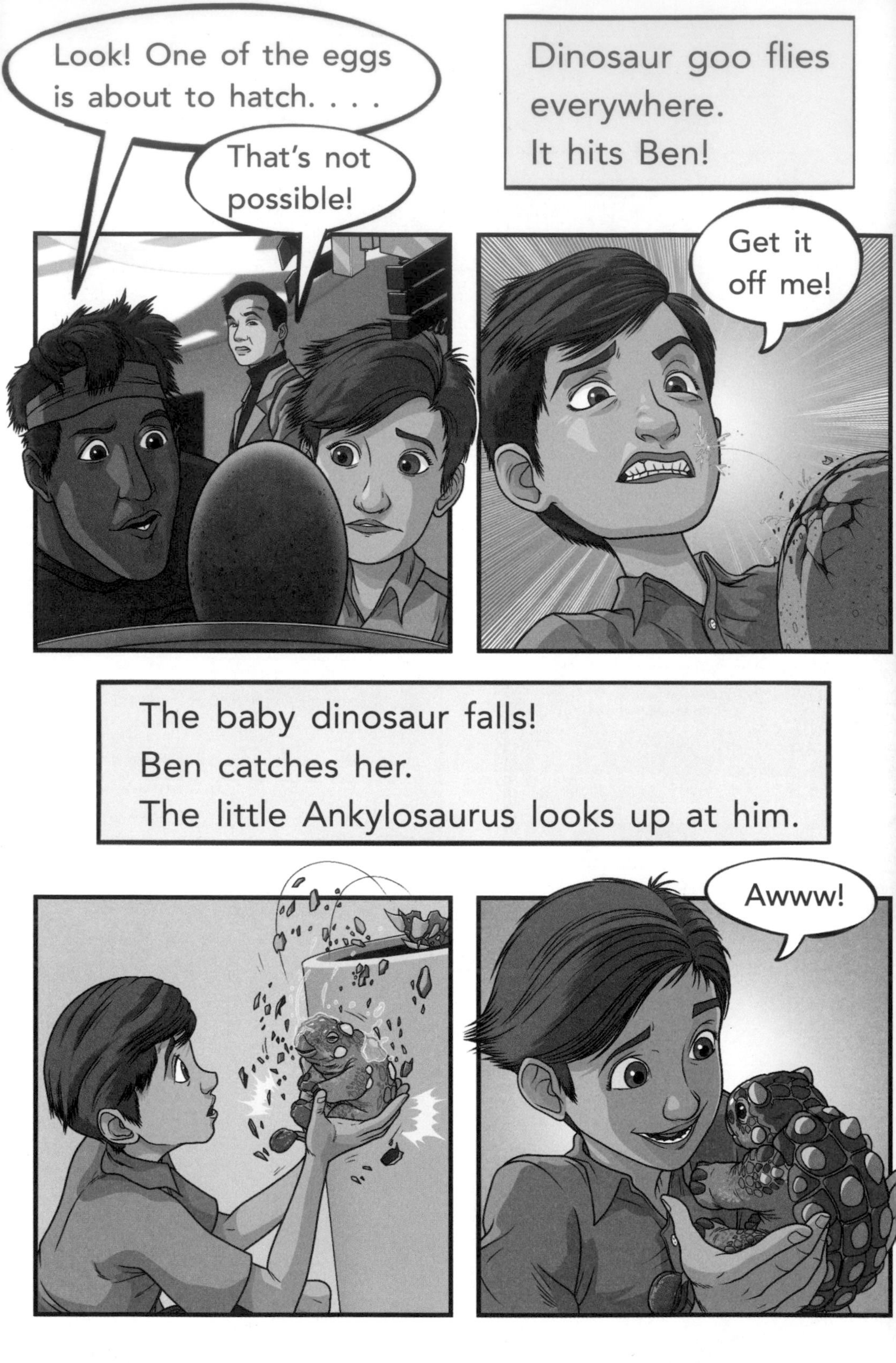

Look! One of the eggs is about to hatch. . . .
That's not possible!
Dinosaur goo flies everywhere.
It hits Ben!
Get it off me!
The baby dinosaur falls!
Ben catches her.
The little Ankylosaurus looks up at him.
Awww!

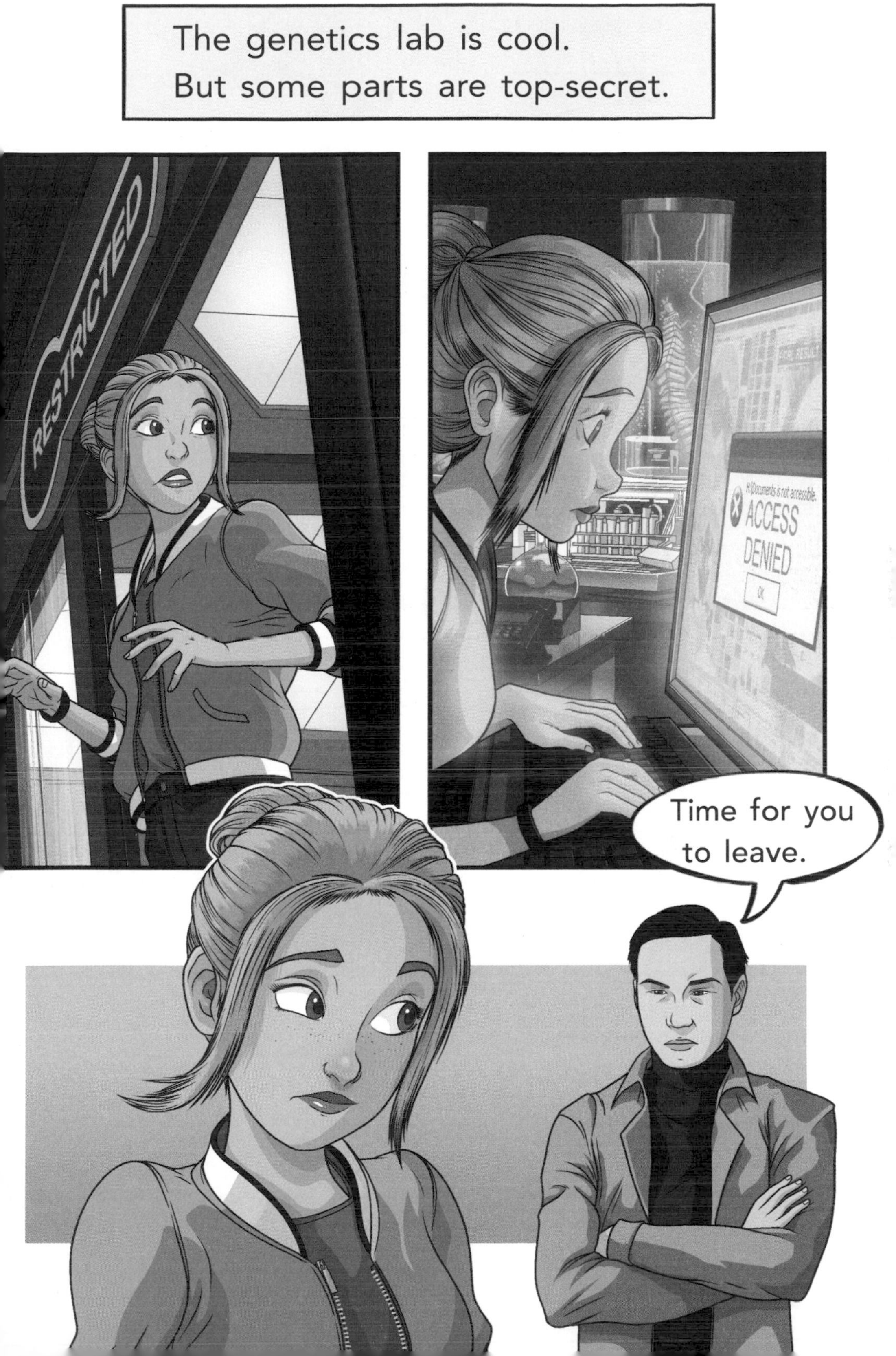
The genetics lab is cool.
But some parts are top-secret.
RESTRICTED
ACCESS DENIED
Time for you to leave.

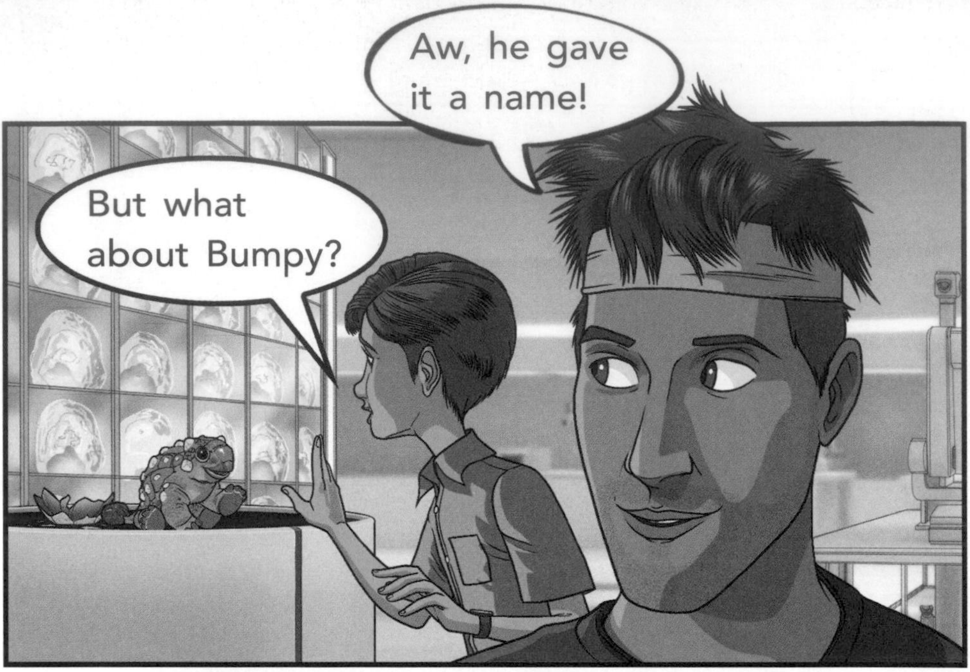
Aw, he gave it a name!
But what about Bumpy?

The kids leave in a hurry. Roxie and Dave remind them of the rules!

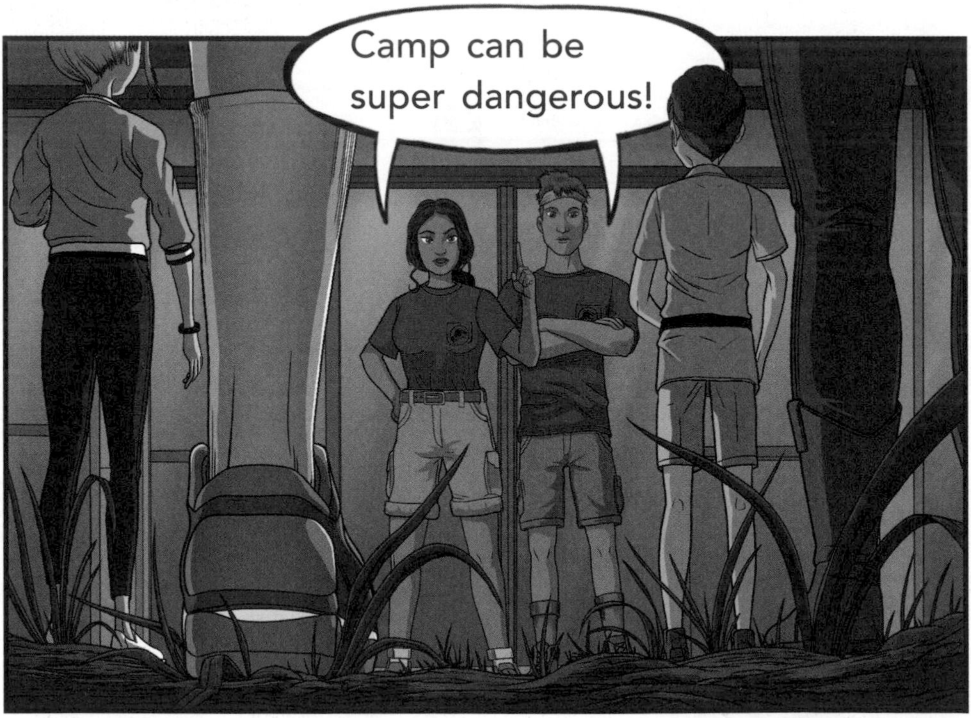
Camp can be super dangerous!

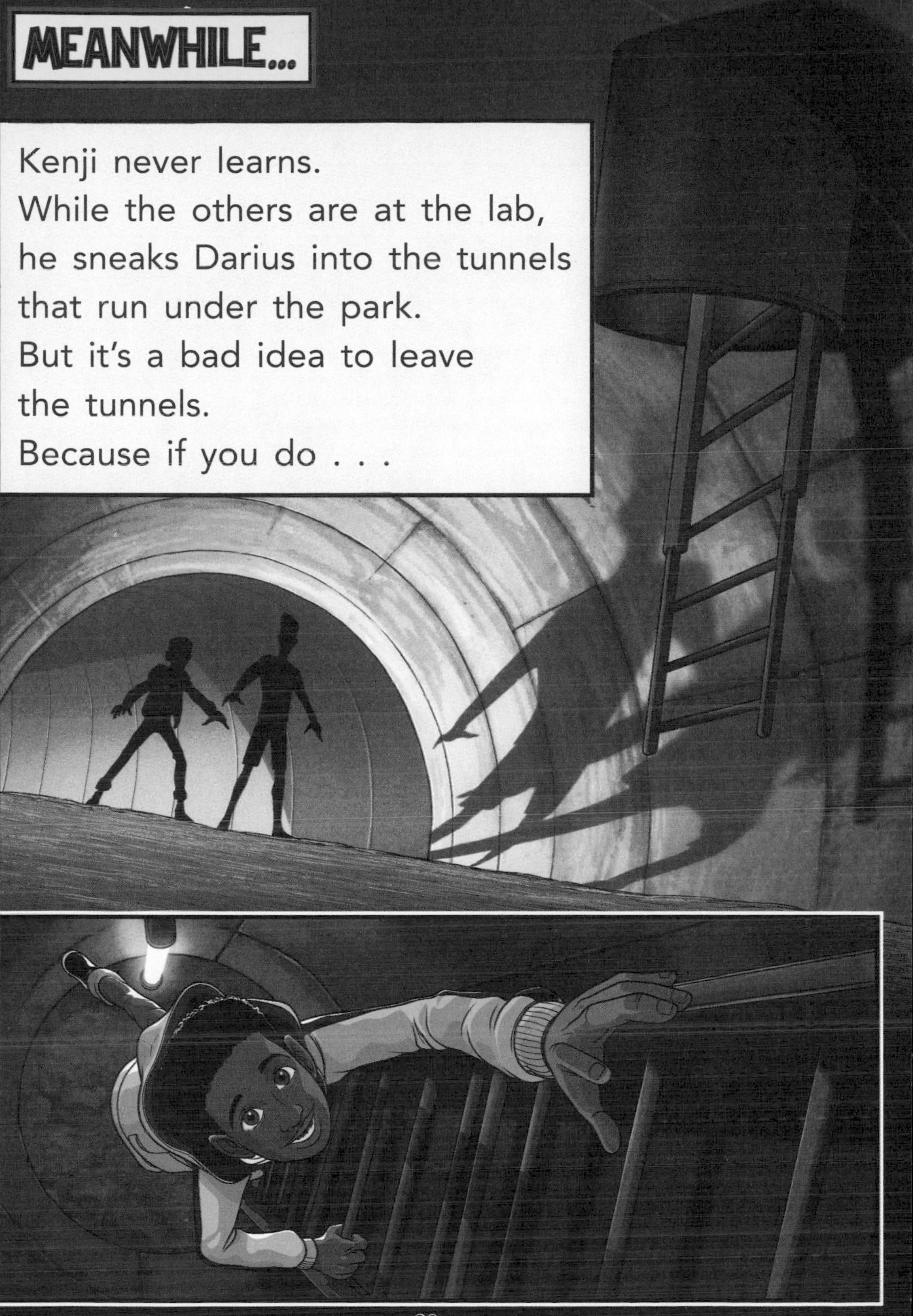
MEANWHILE...
Kenji never learns.
While the others are at the lab,
he sneaks Darius into the tunnels
that run under the park.
But it's a bad idea to leave
the tunnels.
Because if you do . . .

. . . you might find something.
Or something might find you!

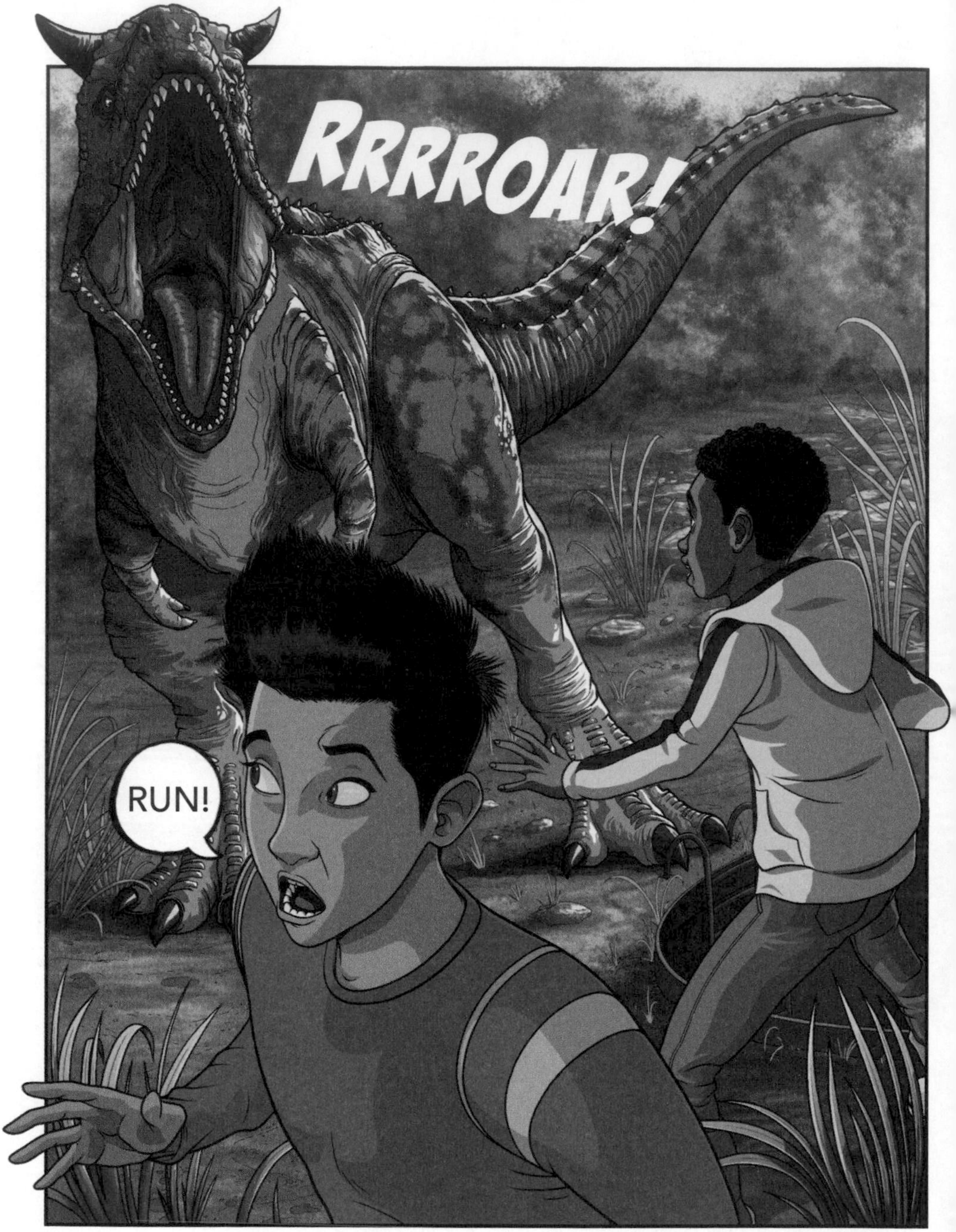
RRRROAR!
RUN!

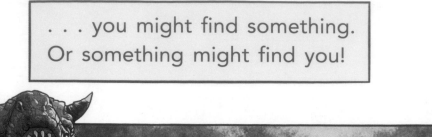

It's been a really long day.
The tired kids meet back at camp.

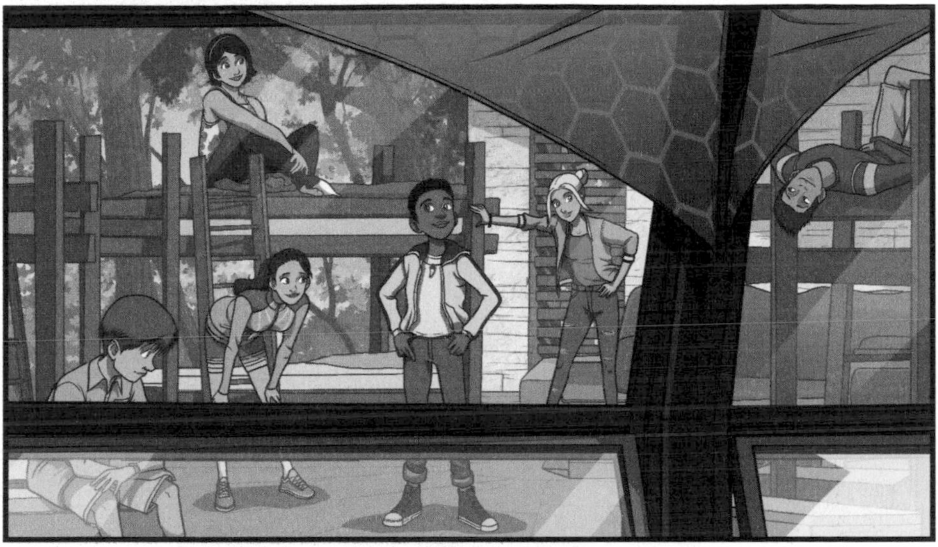

Darius drifts off to sleep
dreaming of dinosaurs.
But the best part is . . .

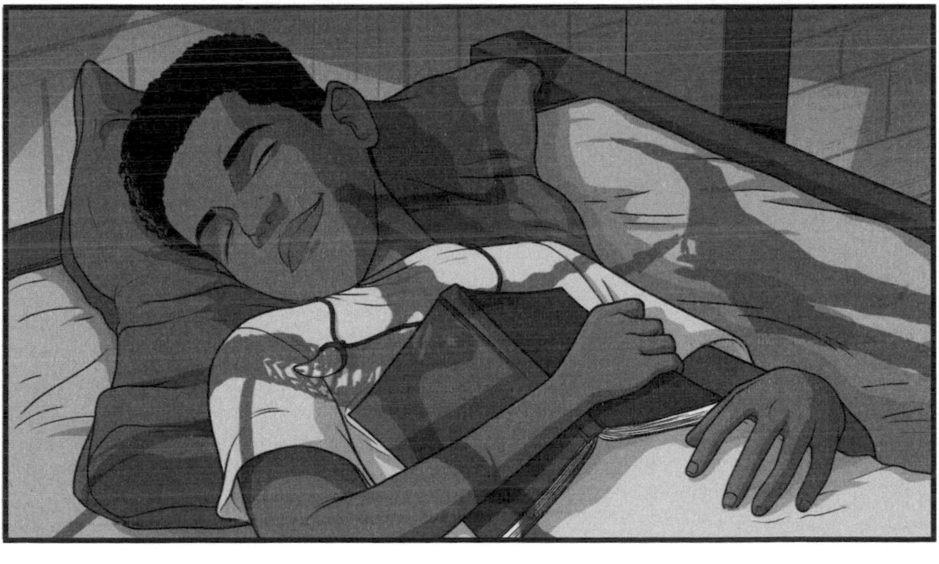

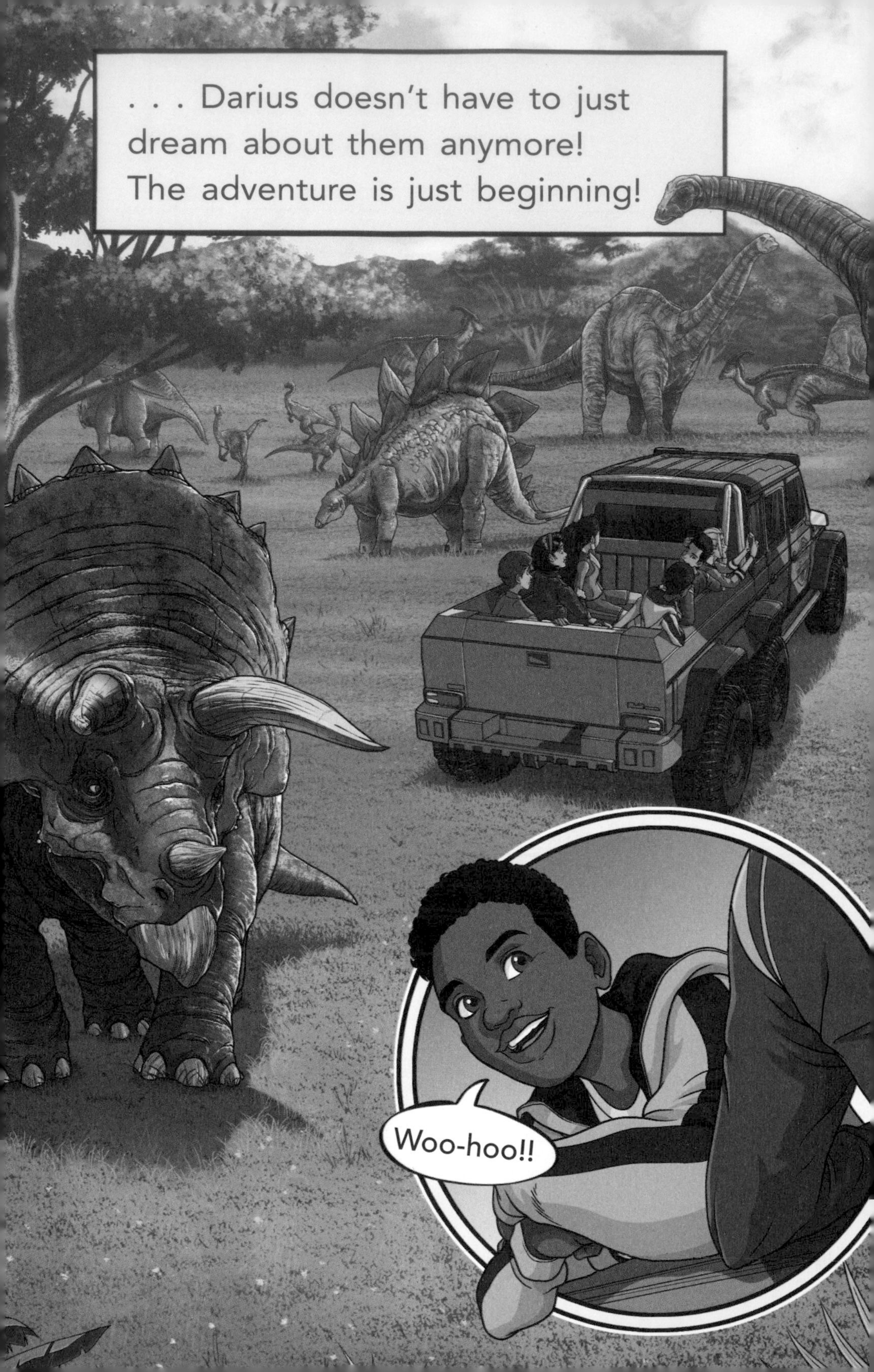
. . . Darius doesn't have to just dream about them anymore! The adventure is just beginning!
Woo-hoo!!